phya

Wormwood

JUL 2016

About the author

Katherine Farmar was born in Dublin and has lived there all her life, apart from a year spent in Edinburgh studying philosophy. *Wormwood Gate* is her first novel.

WORMWOOD GATE

KATHERINE FARMAR

WORMWOOD GATE
Published 2013
by Little Island
7 Kenilworth Park
Dublin 6W
Ireland

www.littleisland.ie

ISBN 978-1-908195-24-1

British Library Cataloguing Data. A CIP catalogue record for this book
is available from the British Library.

Cover design by Pony and Trap.
Typeset in Adobe Caslon by Paul Woods – www.paulthedesigner.ie .

Printed in Poland by Drukarnia Skleniarz.

Little Island receives financial assistance from
The Arts Council (An Chomhairle Ealaíon), Dublin, Ireland.

10 9 8 7 6 5 4 3 2

Dedicated to the memory of Diana Wynne Jones, storyteller supreme.

1

Julie collected place names. Since the age of twelve, she had been keeping a notebook with interesting place names in it; she had started with 'Ballyjamesduff' and 'Timbuktu' because all her life she had been sure they were not real places – just names that somebody had made up for a joke or because they needed a rhyme to fit into a song. Then a priest had come to her school to give a talk about the time he'd spent in Timbuktu and had mentioned in passing that he'd been born in Ballyjamesduff, and Julie felt her world tilt on its axis. It turned out that Ballyjamesduff and Timbuktu were real places, places where people got born and grew up and went to school and caught buses, and somehow that gave their names a kind of magic. To mark the discovery, Julie bought a blank notebook and wrote down each name on a separate page, going back later to add some facts about each place so that she would remember how real they were.

She tried not to tell people about the notebook unless they actually saw her writing in it, because whenever she did tell people, they immediately assumed that she must be very good at geography and usually asked for help with their homework. But a long string of Bs and the occasional C in her own geography homework had culminated in a C in her Junior Cert exam, to everyone's surprise but hers.

'Never mind,' said her friend Tina as the lunchtime bell rang and they started packing their bags to go home. 'Unlike *some* people, you did well in everything else. Oh, hey, don't forget to come to my place at seven tonight! The party's not there, but we're meeting there.'

Julie looked up from her bag. 'Party?' she said, feeling a little stupid for asking. 'What party?'

Tina rolled her eyes. '*The* party. The results party! It'll be a laugh. Everyone legless and celebrating.'

'Wait, I don't remember –'

'J, I've been planning this forever. And you said you'd come months ago. Don't tell me one little C is changing your mind?'

She didn't remember Tina even mentioning a party, much less inviting her to one. She wasn't sure whether to feel grateful to Tina for mentioning it now or annoyed that she hadn't mentioned it before.

'Oh – no, it's not that. I –'

'So you're coming, then?'

'Yes, of course,' said Julie, momentarily letting irritation defeat gratitude. 'But I don't have anything to wear.'

'Oh, well, you should've said!' Tina swung her bag over one arm and linked her other arm with Julie's as they strolled out of the classroom and towards the school gates. 'Let's go shopping!'

'Why do I get the feeling you would have said that even if I didn't need to buy something for the party?'

'You know me too well. We could try that new place in the Stephen's Green Centre.'

'Which place? Oh, wait, I know the one. No, not there. I looked there the other day, and everything they have is beige. No, I want to get something colourful.'

'H&M?'

'Maybe. I was thinking of a dress, but lately all their dresses are, like, micro-micro-minis.'

'What's wrong with that? You have great legs.'

'I do not!'

'You should let people see them once in a while.'

'I get all shy if I wear a short skirt. I feel like I have to tug it down every five minutes or everyone will see my knickers.'

'You say that like it's a bad thing.'

Julie giggled nervously and cast around for another topic. It wasn't that she didn't like the way she looked in short skirts, and it wasn't even that she minded showing off and looking sexy – only, when she dressed a certain way people expected things. *Boys* expected things. It was better not to give them ideas.

As they turned the corner, Tina muttered something and her hand tightened briefly on Julie's arm. Julie followed her gaze to the bus stop, where Aisling O'Riordan was standing, fastening a spiked leather collar around her neck. As they watched, she settled the collar to her satisfaction, took out a lipstick from her schoolbag and began applying it with the aid of a nearby car's wing mirror. Julie couldn't see it clearly from where she was standing, but past experience suggested that the lipstick was probably black. She could feel her face hardening into a scowl.

'Don't,' murmured Tina, as they neared the bus stop.

'Don't *what*?' Julie whispered.

'Don't start anything,' Tina replied.

Julie took a breath to deny that she ever would, then she realised that Aisling could probably hear them by now and shook her head.

Aisling looked back at them. 'Don't worry, girly girls,' she said, capping the (sure enough, black) lipstick and putting it back in her bag. 'I'm waiting for the bus home, but you're going shopping in town, aren't you?'

'Hey!' said Julie. 'Were you eavesdropping on –'

'So you can take this one coming now and you won't have to share a bus with me and pretend to be civil.'

Aisling smiled sweetly and bowed with a gesture worthy of a circus MC as the bus juddered to a halt at the stop. Julie wanted to laugh, wanted to spit, and knowing the joke was on her made her angrier, but somehow it didn't make it less ridiculous. She sucked in a breath, ready to let off a rant, but Tina squeezed her arm again. 'Come on, let's get this one. Bye, Aisling.'

They jumped up the steps and into the bus. While Tina was fumbling for change, Julie glanced back at the stop, and Aisling waved goodbye sarcastically. Julie hadn't even realised that it was possible to put sarcasm into a wave.

Once they'd found seats on the top deck, Tina turned to Julie and spread her hands. 'Well?'

'Well, what?' asked Julie.

'What was that about?'

'Why are you asking me? I don't know what goes on in that weird little head of hers.'

Tina gave her a dubious look. 'You don't exactly ignore her, you know. She wouldn't bait you like that if she didn't think you'd rise to it. Besides, she's harmless enough.'

Julie turned away, breathing out against the window and doodling a little spiral in the fog. 'I suppose.'

'No "I suppose" about it,' said Tina. 'She's a weirdo,

but she hasn't actually *done* anything, has she?'

Julie wiped away the spiral and stared at the dirt on the outside of the window, thinking about Aisling. They had been in the same class for over two years – Aisling had transferred from another school after first year – and right from the start there had been something about Aisling that had nagged at her, made her uncomfortable, made her want either to run away or to lash out. She usually chose to lash out, because running away made her feel like a coward, and when she lashed out, Aisling lashed back, but Aisling had never made the first move, and so far it had all stayed on the level of words. 'No, she hasn't.'

'You should work it out, whatever it is. She's in our class, so you have to put up with her.'

'I know, I know –'

'And I think she's going to be at the party tonight.'

'What? Why?' Julie's head whipped around to face Tina. 'You didn't ask her, did you?'

Tina rolled her eyes. 'As if! Me and Aisling have an arrangement: I ignore her, she ignores me, we're both happy. No, it wasn't me, and anyway it's not my party, it's Darren's.'

'So Darren asked her? Wait, who's Darren?'

'Darren! You know, Caoimhe's fella? With the silver earring?'

Julie had met at least five boys with silver earrings in the past three years, and she had never bothered learning any of their names. She did remember Tina introducing her to a girl called Caoimhe, who had been hanging off the arm of some boy, but the boy himself hadn't registered in her memory. 'Oh, yeah,' she said. 'Does he know Aisling?'

'They're in some World of Warcraft club together or something. He might not have asked her, and if he did she might not have said yes, but I just thought I should warn you.'

'Thanks,' Julie said, sighing. 'I should work on my ignoring-annoying-people skills.'

'Well, anyway,' said Tina after a slightly awkward pause, 'we were going to get you some clothes. If you won't wear a mini, will you at least wear leggings?'

Julie gave a half-smile. 'Leggings I can manage,' she said.

That evening, she spent so long putting on make-up and trying to get her hair-straightener to work the way it was supposed to that she was half an hour late to Tina's place, which made the trip to Darren's house a little tense. Tina didn't believe in being fashionably late. She liked to be early so that she could size people up as they arrived, introduce people to each other, encourage little clusters and knots of people to form in the way that she wanted them to form. No matter who was technically giving the party, any party Tina went to ended up being hers – provided she arrived early enough.

KaTHERINE FARMAR

'I'm *so* sorry,' said Julie for the third time, as they waited at a crossing near Christchurch. It was the worst kind of crossing, with traffic zooming past in five different directions and a road so wide that the pedestrian signals changed when they were only halfway across.

'It's OK,' said Tina, bending her knees in a cha-cha motion to fend off the cold.

Julie thought about making some kind of remark about how Irish people seemed to be biologically incapable of dressing appropriately for cold weather, but Tina was already annoyed. Better to change the subject. 'So, Darren lives … where did you say he lived?'

'Oh, it's this street that's sort of tucked in behind some other streets. I don't know what it's called, but I'll know it when I see it.'

'You've been there before?'

'Yeah.'

'S-so … is he, you know, sound?'

'He's nice enough.'

'Cool.' Julie hugged herself and started rubbing her arms, which were bare. She was wearing floral-pattern leggings (Tina's choice; Julie wasn't sure about them), a long sleeveless T-shirt with a *Sesame Street* design on it (Julie's choice; Tina thought it looked weird), a loose belt slung round her hips, and ballet slippers with pop socks. Even though she was wearing a vest

8

top underneath the shirt (she hadn't told Tina this, of course), she felt underdressed for the weather and a little foolish. Tina had said that a coat would just be a burden later on, when they went to a different party or to a club, but right now Julie felt she'd be happy to put up with lugging a coat around to a dozen different places if only it would stop her from freezing to death.

'This is the oldest part of Dublin, you know,' she said, for lack of anything else to say.

'Oh, yeah?'

'Yeah. The old walls are around here. Well, the bits of them that are left, anyway.'

'I suppose the Vikings landed somewhere near here, then,' Tina said without enthusiasm.

'Yeah, there were archaeological digs that found remains. Old settlements, stuff like that.'

The lights changed, and the girls dashed across the street, not stopping at the traffic islands. By the time they'd reached the other side, they were both too breathless to talk, to Julie's great relief. Tina wasn't really interested in Vikings, and Julie's mind had gone blank on every other possible topic.

They reached the party a few minutes later, and Tina nudged Julie as they were getting drinks in the kitchen. 'See?' she said. 'I told you.'

Sure enough, Aisling was there, stirring a bowl of what might have been fruit punch but, to judge from the fizz, was probably just orange-flavoured alcopops with lemon slices floating on top. Julie felt the familiar discomfort bubbling up in her stomach. She took a deep breath to suppress it and filled a paper cup with Coke, trying not to look in Aisling's direction or draw attention to herself. Aisling didn't say anything, and Julie and Tina were able to get their drinks and leave the kitchen without even saying hello.

Tina bounded into the sitting-room and immediately grabbed hold of a boy Julie didn't recognise and started steering him towards a girl she knew from school. With her Coke in hand, Julie wandered slowly through the room, watching the people: people she knew and people she didn't know, people she'd met before whose names she couldn't remember, people she'd seen around but had never actually been introduced to. That was Darren with the earring and the Slipknot T-shirt, sitting on the arm of the sofa and leaning over a red-haired girl who was definitely not Caoimhe. Privately, Julie made a prediction: by the end of the night, Darren and Caoimhe would have a screaming row, probably on the way to the club. Then there was the boy next to the red-haired girl, who had finished one can of cider and was starting on his second, all the while talking loudly and making the exaggerated gestures of someone who'd drunk five times as much; it wasn't hard to guess that he'd overstep his bounds and end up puking his guts out and having to go home early. And next to him, dressed in black and looking bored, was Aisling, who was staring straight at Julie with an expression of wry sympathy, as if she knew exactly what Julie was thinking.

Julie felt a blush rising on her cheeks and she turned around rapidly before it could show, heading back into the kitchen to the table stacked with snacks and drinks. Maybe she should drink something alcoholic to get into the spirit of things. She hated the taste of beer, and cider wasn't much better, but everyone said that vodka didn't taste of anything, so you could add it to a glass of something sweet and barely notice.

She picked up the bottle of vodka and hefted it in her hand. The seal was broken, but it was almost full. She twisted the cap off and took a sniff. It didn't smell like it would be tasteless. Or odourless, for that matter. It smelled like she'd just about manage to get it down if she added a shot to her Coke, but there was no way she'd be able to hide the smell from her mother.

She put the bottle down.

She headed for the sitting room, nearly bumping into Tina on the way.

'Oh, there you are!' said Tina. 'Listen, there's this guy I want you to meet. He's really nice, you'll like him!'

Julie narrowed her eyes. 'Are you matchmaking again?'

Tina put her hand on her chest. 'Me? Matchmaking? Would I do that?'

'You don't want me to answer that, do you?'

'Not really. Come on, he's in here.'

'Oh … well, I suppose it won't do any harm.'

Julie let herself be led towards a pleasant-looking boy with a floppy fringe and a beer in his hand. Apparently his name was Kevin and he was at the same school as Darren, though not in the same class, and he had done much better at the exams than he'd expected, which was great, because his parents had promised him a gift of €100 for every A.

'I wish my parents were that generous,' said Julie. 'The most I can expect from them if I do well is warm approval.'

'Heh. So how did you do, then?' said Kevin.

Julie could feel her smile freezing. 'Could we talk about something else?' she said. 'I mean, I don't … it's not that I –'

'Well, like … like what?'

'Anything! God, I'm just so glad to get those things behind me, I don't have to think about them ever again! I don't want to talk about them!' Julie could hear her voice growing shrill and she took a deep breath to calm herself. 'I mean, we spent three years working towards the Junior Cert, and now it's over, right, so we don't have to talk about it any more. We don't even have to think about it. So could we talk about … I don't know. Politics. Films. Have you read any good books lately?'

Kevin looked at her warily. 'Last thing I read was *Arthas: Rise of the Lich-King*,' he said. 'It's a WoW tie-in.'

'Wow?'

'You know, World of Warcraft? Do you play?'

'Ah … no,' said Julie, her heart sinking. She had only the vaguest notion of what World of Warcraft was, and she had the awful suspicion that she'd offended Kevin irretrievably; a suspicion that was only confirmed when their conversation limped on for another couple of minutes before Kevin spotted somebody across the room he wanted to talk to and excused himself. Julie sat alone for a minute, her right foot jogging up and down nervously, then finished off her Coke in one long swallow and asked the nearest person where the bathroom was.

Once she found it, she bolted the door and leaned against it, her eyes closed and her hands pressed against her face. *It's me*, she thought. *I'm the problem. Everyone else is having a fine time. What's wrong with me?*

She let her hands fall and thought of Aisling, who had seemed to understand – had seemed to know what was going on in Julie's head without being told. That didn't seem fair, to be so transparent, and to somebody she didn't even like.

Somebody knocked on the door.

'I'll be out in a minute!' Julie said, and she scurried

over to the toilet, which she flushed, not wanting people to think she'd been hogging the bathroom for no reason. She ran water over her hands and patted her face carefully, trying not to smudge her make-up, then composed her best cheerful expression with the aid of the mirror, and breezed back out into the party.

The trickle of new guests had dwindled to nothing, and Darren was looking restless. Julie cast her eyes around until they lit on Caoimhe, who was sitting by the stereo fiddling with CDs. 'Hiya,' she said.

Caoimhe glanced up and said, 'Oh, hi,' then let her eyes drop again. It looked like she was trying to avoid looking at Darren.

'Think we'll be heading out soon?' Julie said in a low voice.

Caoimhe looked up. 'That's a good idea,' she said. 'It's early yet, but there were others that were going to come, only I don't think they're coming here. I think they thought we were going to meet at the club.'

'Have you tried texting them?'

'Yeah, but nothing's getting sent. I reckon the networks are overloaded tonight, with the night that's in it. Almost as bad as New Year's Eve.'

She looked over at Darren then, and Julie followed her gaze; Darren was still next to the red-haired girl, fidgeting and looking around but somehow never meeting Caoimhe's eyes. *I give it twenty minutes*, Julie thought. *And even odds that she hits him.*

Darren stood up, slapping his thighs. 'Right, lads, will we go soon? I don't think there's any point waiting for Fitzer and that lot. If they're not here now, they won't be here tonight.'

There was a rustle and rumble of agreement and shuffling feet. Caoimhe turned off the music and stalked over to Darren. Julie turned her face away to hide a smile and trotted upstairs to get her bag from the pile of bags and coats in the spare bedroom before there was a rush. There was an ankle-length black leather coat on the top of the pile. She felt her mouth twisting as she looked at it, and she pushed it aside to pull her bag out from underneath it. The leather felt smooth and supple under her fingers, and she couldn't resist picking the coat up and hefting it in her hands. It was just as heavy as she'd thought it would be, but when she settled it around her shoulders it felt strangely comforting, more like a hug from strong arms than a heavy bag.

'Thinking of changing your look?'

Julie slipped the coat off and back onto the bed and twirled around, scowling, in the hope that a fierce expression would hide her embarrassment. 'How do you wear that thing?' she snapped. 'I bet it makes you look like a drug dealer.'

Aisling smirked. 'How do you wear *that* stuff? Don't you freeze to death?'

'I'm not a Goth, unlike some people, so I have actual body heat.'

Aisling's smirk faded. 'Hey, who are you calling a Goth?'

Julie stared pointedly at Aisling's T-shirt, which was black and long-sleeved and decorated with an intricate swirling pattern featuring the word GOTH in large silvery letters.

Aisling looked down at it and shrugged, unmoved. 'It's *ironic*,' she said.

Despite herself, Julie laughed. Aisling frowned, but the edges of her mouth were twitching. 'Anyway, gimme my coat. We're off to some stupid nightclub or other, and *unlike some people* I actually care about staying warm.'

Julie picked the coat back up and handed it to her. 'See you,' she said, pushing past Aisling and out of the room.

It was weird, talking to Aisling like they had something in common.

The party guests took another twenty minutes to gather their belongings and finally leave – time Julie spent lurking in a corner near where Tina was talking to some boy whose name she couldn't remember. When they got going, Julie tried to stay close to Tina, but Tina flashed her a warning look, and the little laugh and head-tilt she offered to the boy a moment later was so obviously her Flirt Mode signal that Julie found she didn't even want to keep walking by her side. Tina got so boring when she was interested in somebody. It was as if her brain was a hard drive and boys were magnets.

She slowed her pace to let Tina and the boy overtake her, and let herself drift to the back of the group. Much to her discomfort, she found herself walking a little in front of Aisling, who had taken up the rearmost position. Well, that didn't have to mean that they'd talk to each other. They could walk on the same pavement without speaking. People did it all the time.

'Oh, hey there,' said Aisling. 'Got dumped for a boy?'

So much for that theory.

'None of your business.'

'Suit yourself.'

There was a pause, and Julie allowed herself to hope that it would last until they reached the club.

'So, do you know what club we're going to?'

No such luck.

'Em …' A few names had been mentioned, but Julie wasn't sure which was the right one. 'No.'

'Not that it matters,' said Aisling, as if Julie hadn't spoken at all, 'since they're all pretty much the same. A DJ playing Top 40 hits and a bunch of wankers in white shirts and a bouncer with an attitude problem.'

Julie stopped dead. 'Why do you come to these things if you're so above it all?' she said, spitting out the words. 'Why do you act like you've seen everything and you know better than everyone? You're the same age as the rest of us, but you act like you're a thousand years old and you're all … all world-weary and … and jaded. But you're not!'

Aisling, who had stopped as well, folded her arms slowly across her chest. 'I'm not into this stuff. It doesn't appeal to me. So it bores me. I get bored. I'm not pretending I know anything I don't know. I just know one thing really well: I'm not having fun. That's all I need to know.'

'If you don't have any fun, why bother coming?' Julie asked. 'What are you even doing here?'

Aisling raised one eyebrow, which gave Julie a momentary pang of envy; she'd always wanted to be able to do that, and she'd never managed it, not even after hours of practice in front of a mirror.

'I'm here because Darren is a mate of mine and he wanted me to be here. But I could ask you the same question.'

'What? Don't be ridiculous!'

Aisling lowered her hands to her hips. 'Are you going to claim that you were having fun? I saw you, OK? I saw that look on your face. You're just as bored as me, you just pretend not to be!'

'I am not! God, this is exactly what I was talking about! You think you know everything? You don't know anything about me!'

'I know you're cold right now. I know Tina picked out those leggings for you –'

'What the … Were you *following* us? You –'

'No, you idiot! I know that because those leggings are exactly Tina's style! I don't know why you're so determined to dress just like her. She's not exactly Anna Wintour.'

'Oh, and I suppose your style is so incredibly individual, Little Miss I'm-Expressing-Myself-By-Dressing-Exactly-Like-All-My-Stupid-Spookykid-Mates!'

'Oh, *piss off*!' Aisling turned on her heel and stomped away, a gesture made more dramatic by her heavy boots and swinging coat-tails, and less so by the fact that Julie immediately sprang forward to follow her.

'Hit a sore spot, did I?'

'I was wrong,' Aisling said, lengthening her stride so that Julie had to scurry to keep up with her. 'I thought maybe we could have a civil conversation for once, but evidently that was too optimistic of me.'

'Civil?' Julie snorted. 'You call that civil? Hey, stop! I'm talking to you!'

Aisling stopped and whirled around to face her. 'You're the one who started with the insults!'

'Started? The first thing you said to me was that I'd been dumped!'

'What? That wasn't – that was a joke! And anyway, it's not like you and Tina are –'

'It was still mean.' Julie cringed to hear herself use that word. *Mean*. As if she were five years old again. 'Anyway, I don't get why you're so sensitive. What have you got to be sensitive about? Are they rounding up the Goths into labour camps now?'

'I … you …' Aisling's mouth was twitching. She covered it with her hand, but it was no good. Julie could see, and hear, that she was laughing, and she couldn't help herself; she had to laugh too. It was curiously calming.

Aisling shrugged, looking embarrassed, and glanced around. 'Hey,' she said, 'I think we've lost them.'

'Lost them? What do you – oh!' There was no sign of the others, and Aisling and Julie were near a three-way junction. 'Arsebiscuits. Do you have Darren's number?'

Aisling flashed her phone's screen at Julie. 'Way ahead of you.' She called a number while Julie bounced up and down on her feet and rubbed her arms to keep warm. 'Huh,' she said after a minute, 'no signal.'

'Oh, I think Caoimhe was talking about that. The networks are clogged or something. Here, I'll try calling Tina. Maybe my provider's having better luck.'

She fished her phone out of her bag and checked the display: no signal. Just in case, she tried calling, but that didn't work either.

'No joy?'

'Nope.'

'Well, if it was just me I'd say this was the perfect excuse to go home and watch *True Blood*, but I'm guessing you'd rather join the others, right?'

Julie nodded. 'But I don't know where they're going.'

'If we head for the quays, we might bump into them. And we might get a signal closer to the centre of town.'

'OK.' Julie nodded and started walking as briskly as possible in what she was pretty sure was the direction of the quays.

For a few paces, she was on her own, and it had just occurred to her to wonder whether Aisling really was going to go home and watch TV when she heard a swish and a creak by her side. 'You don't have to come with me,' she said. 'You could tell Darren you got lost on the way to the club and went home. It's true too.'

'I don't feel like going home just yet,' said Aisling. 'Besides, are you sure you want to be on your own?'

Julie scowled and folded her arms tightly across her chest. 'I'm fine.'

'It's getting dark –'

'It's not that late.'

'But town's going to be really crowded, and –' Aisling sighed. 'Look, if you really want to get rid of me, that's fine. Just let me give you Darren's number so you can call him if you get a signal.'

Julie wasn't sure she did want to get rid of Aisling, not now that they were being kind of … almost … not

21

nice, exactly, but at least friendly to each other. But she wasn't sure if she could say that without looking foolish, so she stopped walking and fished her phone out again. 'Still no signal. Show it to me?'

Aisling handed over her phone, the screen showing her contact list. 'Thanks,' said Julie, keying in Darren's number. She accidentally scrolled down the contact list when she was done and saw a number saved under 'This Phone'. 'You have your own number in your contacts?' she said, disbelieving.

Aisling shrugged. 'I never have to phone myself, so I can never remember my own number. Then when I have to tell people… it's just easier. You should put my number in, actually,' she added. 'Just in case. And I should get yours.'

'OK,' said Julie, 'just a sec.' She keyed in Aisling's number and then handed Aisling her own phone. Aisling took it with a small smile, adding Julie's number to her contacts with quick, deft movements of her thumb, and Julie was on the verge of saying … she wasn't sure what, but something that would make Aisling change her mind about splitting up, when a sharp smell came out of nowhere, forcing its way down her throat and nostrils and making her gag. 'Urgh! What is that?'

Aisling was pinching her nose and had her hands over her mouth. 'I ihn ih brumbud,' she said through her fingers.

Julie's hand rose to cover her own nose, but the smell had faded as quickly as it had arisen. 'What did you say?'

Aisling let go of her nose and sniffed the air cautiously, then let both her hands drop. 'I think it's wormwood,' she says. 'Which is bizarre, because it's not like a lot of people grow wormwood in this part of town. Or anywhere.'

'Wormwood? What is wormwood?'

'It's a herb. They use it to make absinthe.'

'Stands to reason you'd know about it, then. Maybe somebody broke an absinthe bottle.'

Aisling frowned. 'That wouldn't –' Her head jerked around, and she pointed up to a street sign two storeys above the ground. 'Heeeey, look at that!'

'Wormwood Gate,' said Julie, savouring the way the words felt in her mouth. 'Oh, that's a good one.' She rummaged in her bag for the notebook and pencil she always brought with her. 'Got to write this one down.'

'Don't you think it's weird?' said Aisling. 'We're on a street called Wormwood Gate, and we just happen to get a smell of wormwood?'

'It's a coincidence,' said Julie, writing *WORMWOOD GATE (street) (Dublin, Ireland)* on the head of a fresh page. She'd add the historical details later, when she'd had a chance to look them up. 'The name probably doesn't even mean "wormwood",' she added. 'Place names change all the time. I mean … there used to be a wall around the city, in this part of town. The wall must have had gates, right? And one of them was here.'

'That doesn't make it any less spooky,' said Aisling. 'Come on! It may be a coincidence, but it's a cool coincidence! Don't you think?'

Julie stuffed her notebook and pencil back into her bag, exasperated. 'I think –'

But she never got a chance to say what she thought, because at that very moment a door opened in the air in front of them and a white horse with a red mane galloped through at full speed, bowling them over onto the ground.

2

Julie stared up at the sky, too winded to speak or move. Her heart was pounding in her chest like a kettle drum, and she was having trouble breathing. *The light*, she thought. *The light is all wrong.*

'Are you all right?' said Aisling. Her voice sounded worried, and somehow smaller than before, as if the two of them were at opposite ends of a very long tunnel. Julie tried to speak, but all that came out was a squeaky rasp of breath. She pulled herself to a sitting position, brushed some grit off her palms, cleared her throat, and tried again.

'I'm fine,' she said.

'You look like you've seen a ghost,' said Aisling.

Julie looked at Aisling's face. It should have been hard to tell what she looked like, whether she was pale or blushing or the same as usual. She shouldn't have been able to see much in the orange glow of the streetlights. But she could see every detail, from the black streak where her eyeliner had gotten smudged to the little red bump on her chin where a zit was about to form. She looked pale but, considering the way she wore her make-up, that might have been perfectly normal.

'What just happened?' said Julie. Her heart was beginning to slow down now, and she felt like maybe she might be strong enough to stand up without falling over. She tried it, leaning on Aisling's shoulder without asking, and took a look around.

'Jesus *Christ*,' she said, and fell again.

'It would probably be good if you stopped doing that,' said Aisling, and her voice didn't sound distant any more, but it did sound shaky, as if she was trying not to cry.

'I'm not doing it on purpose,' said Julie. 'Look, help me up this time and maybe I'll be all right.'

Aisling grunted at that, but took hold of Julie's hands anyway and half-pulled her upright. Julie leaned on her and looked around again, trying to make what she was seeing fit into her brain.

The ground beneath their feet was not concrete or tarmac, but cobblestones, and the clouds above their heads glowed red, not orange; not reflecting sodium lights but what seemed to be a massive fire – no, two fires – no, *three* fires, one of them very close to where they were standing. There was still a river to their left, but when Julie rushed towards it to get a better view of what lay along the quays, she saw at once that it was not the Liffey. Couldn't be. It was narrow, and the water was clean, and there were seals frolicking around in it, their heads bobbing under and over the surface. There were no bridges, either, that she could see.

'What the hell?' she said.

'I think,' said Aisling slowly, in a low voice, as if she were talking to herself, 'that somebody slipped me something, and this is a hallucination. At least, that seems like a reasonable hypothesis, given the evidence.'

'If you're hallucinating, what am I doing here?'

'Well, you must be a figment of my imagination.'

Julie glared at her. The leather coat was so thick that pinching her arm would have no effect, and the big stompy boots she was wearing probably had steel toecaps, so she grabbed Aisling's hand and twisted her arm back.

'OW!' Aisling cried. 'What the hell are you doing? Let go!'

'Ever get your arm twisted in a dream?'

'That's hardly a reason to –'

'Nobody slipped you anything, Aisling. You're really here, wherever "here" is, and so am I.' She let go of Aisling's hand. 'Look at those seals!'

Aisling stared, looking a little dazed. 'I saw a seal from the top deck of the bus once,' she said slowly. 'I couldn't believe what I was seeing. A seal, in the Liffey? It had to be lost.'

'There's a whole family of them, look.'

'I see them.'

'You're not even looking in the right direction!'

'I'm looking past them. What's that thing? It looks like – don't you think it looks like – here, look –' She pointed, and Julie looked away from the seals to where her finger was aiming. 'Don't you think it looks like …'

'Like a … horse?' Julie said. 'It's coming this way. It's swimming! I didn't know horses could swim.'

Aisling looked at her, frowning. 'They can't,' she said. 'Well, they can, but not far, and not in water this deep.' She looked back at the probably-a-horse's-head. 'It's bobbing around at a weird angle, don't you think?'

Julie shrugged. The probably-a-horse's-head had come quite close; if it had been a person, she could have shouted to it.

'I don't know what a swimming horse is supposed to look like,' she said.

'I'm not a horse,' said the creature in a great big booming voice, swimming towards them all the while. 'I'm a merhorse, and I can't help but wonder what two such creatures as you are doing in the City of the Three Castles.'

Julie blinked and glanced at Aisling, whose face

had gone quite blank. 'The City of the Three Castles?' she said. 'Is that what this place is called?'

The creature stopped where it was in the water and stared up at them. It occurred to Julie that, although it looked as if it was just standing still, the river was deep and fast enough that it must have been swimming quite strongly against the current just to avoid being swept away. 'Not just two-legs, but mortal two-legs,' it said, as if it were talking to itself. 'Well, well, I suppose there's no help for it.'

'Can you tell us where this place is?' said Julie. 'I've never heard of the City of the Three Castles before.'

The merhorse huffed, a sound somewhere between a laugh and a snort. 'The City is in the Kingdom of Crows,' it said, then shook its head a little. 'Well, no, strictly speaking it's not any more. It was once, you see, but it's been part of the Realms Between for … I'm not sure how long, but a good long while. Though not so long that the Queen-that-is ever stops worrying about the Queen of Crows stealing the City back.'

'That doesn't actually clear anything up,' Aisling muttered.

Julie gave her a dig in the ribs, but the merhorse kept talking as if it hadn't heard.

'You'll be wanting to get back, I suppose,' it said. 'Well, you needn't ask me for help, for I have nothing to do with the gates or the roads or any of that nonsense. I stay in the River with the seals and the souls, and here I am quite content.'

'When you say "get back" …'

Julie hesitated. It wasn't that she was entirely taking what she was seeing at face value. There was a part of her brain that was screaming and gibbering inside at the weirdness of it; but that part wasn't the part that was in control.

'Get back to where you came from, of course,' said the merhorse. 'Mortals like you never stay long in the Realms Between. Never seen a one of you stay long enough for a body to have a chat, now that I think of it. Usually you slip in and out in half a breath, just long enough to give the place some atmosphere. But that was before the queen had the gates closed.'

'Wait,' said Julie. 'If the gates are closed, how did we get here?'

'To judge by the smell, you came through the Wormwood Gate,' said the merhorse, and Julie's head snapped around to look at Aisling, who was already looking at her with eyes wide as saucers. 'The Wormwood Gate's not under the queen's control,' the merhorse went on, 'though not for lack of trying on her part. And for all I know, it's gone a-wandering off beyond the bounds of the City by now. It doesn't stay in one place, you see. You might as well go for a stroll through the streets and see if you can find it, though you should keep away from the queen's guards. They'll clap you in irons as soon as lay eyes on you.'

'Thanks for the advice,' said Julie.

'Don't mention it,' said the merhorse, and it leapt up into the air like a dolphin, giving Julie and Aisling a brief glimpse of its scaly, fishy netherparts before it plunged under the water and was gone.

'Oh,' said Aisling, 'a *mer*horse. I get it now.'

'Don't you think it looked familiar?' said Julie tentatively, not quite sure whether she'd just been imagining it. She was not quite sure whether she'd just imagined everything that had happened since they'd left the house, but she was trying not to dwell on that.

Aisling turned around and leaned her elbows on the parapet. 'Yes,' she said, a dreamy expression on her face, 'but not like I'd seen it before in person. More like it was in a painting I saw once, a long time ago.'

Julie opened her mouth to speak but changed her mind and turned around herself, leaning on the parapet just like Aisling. What she could see of the City of the Three Castles was old-looking, in a way. The nearby houses were Georgian, like the old parts of Dublin, all red brick and fanlights and tall sash windows with lots of small panes; but the houses themselves looked new, without a trace of pollution stains or braces in the walls or worn-down brickwork, and farther down the river she could see buildings that looked both older still – Tudor, to judge from the beams – and newer still, as if they had been built yesterday.

She slid her hands sideways and gripped the stone of the parapet. It was granite, rough and solid, with little flecks of mica sparkling in the firelight.

'We're in the City of the Three Castles,' said Aisling, still sounding dreamy and far away.

'Yes,' said Julie.

'In the Realms Between,' said Aisling.

'Yes.'

'Formerly of the Kingdom of Crows.'

'Yes.'

'Shouldn't you be writing this down?'

Julie looked at her. The dreaminess wasn't entirely gone, but the fear and the confusion that had been in her eyes before were nowhere to be seen. Now she looked thoughtful, and perhaps even determined, as if there was something she very much wanted to do.

'You sound pretty calm,' said Julie. 'What happened?'

'I just had a conversation with a merhorse,' said Aisling.

'Hey, I was the one who did the talking! You were too busy freaking out.'

'Well, exactly. Whatever's happening – and I'm not ruling out the possibility that this is an unusually coherent hallucination – wouldn't it be stupid to run around all "Like, oh my God, oh my God, *oh my gaaahd*, I am, like, *so* totally freaked out right now"?'

'Nobody talks like that,' Julie muttered. Aisling gave her a pointed look, and Julie resisted the urge to squirm. All right, maybe she did talk like that sometimes, but only when she'd been hanging out with Tina and the girls and they'd been laughing and getting hyper, and who'd made Aisling 'Polysyllables' O'Riordan the boss of how people should talk, anyway?

'I'm just saying,' said Aisling. '*Carpe diem* and all that. Here we are, right now, wherever "here" is. Let's enjoy the ride. We can freak out later.'

At that, the part of Julie's brain that had been gibbering and screaming fell silent abruptly, and she smiled despite herself. 'That sounds like a plan,' she said, and she laughed. 'This is better than a nightclub!'

Aisling grinned. 'You're telling me!' She grabbed Julie's arms. 'Let's explore! We're going to have to go back sooner or later, but in the mean time, let's see what other weird crap this place has got to offer.'

Julie stepped back, pulling her arms from Aisling's grip but linking her left arm with Aisling's right. 'Lay on, MacDuff. Where should we go first?'

'Well, actually …' Aisling said slowly, a thoughtful look on her face, 'I wasn't kidding when I said you should be writing this down. You write down the places you've been, don't you?'

'Oh!' Julie took out her notebook and pencil and turned to a new page. *CITY OF THE THREE CASTLES*, she wrote on the top of the page, and underneath that *(city) (Realms Between [formerly Kingdom of Crows])*. 'Not that I have any idea what that means,' she said. 'It sounds good, though.'

'Perfect,' said Aisling. 'Now, where do you want to go?'

Julie tucked the notebook and pencil away and looked around. Over the tops of the buildings, she could see a tall tower ringed with white lights somewhere on the other side of the river. It looked majestic.

'How about we go towards that tower?' she said. 'It looks interesting, don't you think?'

'It looks like a good place to start.' Aisling set forth in the direction of the river's flow, a light of purpose shining in her eyes. 'There has to be a bridge along here somewhere,' she said as Julie scrambled to catch up with her. 'Unless everyone in this city is a sea creature. But that doesn't seem likely.'

'Maybe most of them can fly,' said Julie, and Aisling flashed her a grin, her eyes shining even more than before.

Even though the air was just as cold as it had been in Dublin, Julie felt quite warm as she walked alongside the river, alongside Aisling. *This is an adventure,* she thought to herself. She started bouncing on her toes and humming. *A proper adventure!*

Aisling's grin disappeared, replaced by a disapproving scowl. 'What is that you're humming?'

'Oh, you know what it is. Everyone knows!' Just to annoy her further, Julie started actually singing the words and doing a little dance with hops and twirls.

'Shut up!'

'Make me!'

They were passing by streetlights now, but they weren't like normal streetlights: their standards were black and elaborately decorated, and the lights themselves were more like huge candle flames than orange sodium lamps. Aisling glanced at one as they passed it, frowning, but whatever she was thinking was immediately displaced by Julie singing and dancing in a circle around her.

'No, seriously, stop that,' Aisling said. 'It's unbelievably annoying.'

'Would you prefer Justin Bieber?'

Aisling's glare grew sharper. 'Don't even joke about that!'

'Ooh, did I touch a nerve? Are you a closet Belieber? Is that your dark secret?'

'You know, I take it back. I think I prefer –'

'Or One Direction, maybe?'

'Ugh, God, no. I'd prefer that vapid electropop you were singing to that.'

'Lady Gaga is not vapid!'

'The fact that you can even say that with a straight face says terrible things about your experience of music.'

'Oh, stop being such a snob. Anyway, I have lots of experience of music!'

'Sure you do.'

'I take requests! Name a song. Go on, name one!'

Aisling sighed heavily and crossed her arms across her chest. Julie stopped dancing and walked quietly at Aisling's side for a few paces before blurting out, 'I just feel like singing, that's all.'

Aisling uncrossed her arms, and for a few more paces they walked in silence. Aisling wordlessly handed Julie back her phone, and Julie muttered 'Thanks.' She'd forgotten Aisling had it.

'Do you know anything by The Gossip?' said Aisling after a while. 'Or Fall Out Boy? Or Dimmu Borgir?'

'Who?'

'Yeah, didn't think so.'

'Well, obviously I have to know the song if I'm going to sing it. Come on, name a band I've heard of!'

Aisling gave her a look that, if it had been anyone else, Julie would have called "fond". 'It doesn't matter as long as you don't torture my eardrums.'

'You're too closed-minded. You need to –' Julie fell silent. Something had occurred to her, and she grabbed Aisling's elbow.

'Shh! Listen a minute.'

Aisling gave her a puzzled look but cocked her head to listen anyway. They stood like that, as still as statues, until Aisling pulled her elbow from Julie's hand and shrugged expansively.

'What did you hear?' Aisling asked.

'Nothing. Isn't it spooky?'

'What do you … ? Oh!'

Aisling glanced around, and Julie could tell she was noticing what she herself had noticed a moment before: that there were no people on the quays, either on their side of the river or the other side, either walking or in cars or on bikes. There were no sounds of traffic or conversation – no sounds at all except a faint crackling from the lamps and a fainter *zssh zssh* sound as the river lapped against the stone of the banks.

'No boats on the river either,' Julie murmured, suddenly conscious of the silence surrounding them.

Aisling swallowed. 'What say we put off going to the tower and see if we can find some people?' she whispered.

'How do you suggest we do that?' Julie replied, also whispering. 'The only living things we've seen so far have been the seals and the whatchamacallit … merhorse. And it said m-mortals –' Her tongue tripped on the word as if her brain had only just caught up to the implications it carried. She took a slow breath and carried on, '– it said mortals don't usually stay long here.'

'Well, but … there've got to be other people around, right? Not "mortals", whatever that means. We could knock on some doors. Those buildings can't all be empty, can they?'

Julie turned her back to the river and swept her gaze up and down the strip of buildings along the quay.

They didn't have many windows, and the windows they had were mostly pretty small, but some of them were lit up, and there was smoke coming from a few of the chimneys.

'All right,' she whispered. 'But let's be prepared to … I don't know what … to run like mad if anything happens, OK?'

'I'm prepared,' Aisling whispered. 'I'm not going to let any kind of ghoulie or ghostie or long-leggedy beastie get me. And by the way, why are we whispering?'

'I don't know,' said Julie in a normal voice. 'It just seemed appropriate.'

Aisling grinned. 'I'm glad you have a sense of atmosphere. That's going to make this adventure a lot more colourful.'

Julie turned her head to hide a smile; at the word 'adventure', she had felt warmth blooming in her belly.

She strode out for the nearest building she could see with a lit window, not bothering to check whether Aisling was following, and stared long and hard at the door. It was large, wooden, dark with age and reinforced with strips of metal, like something from a medieval castle. It had a big black lock and what looked like a giant peephole. It also had a knocker in the shape of a merhorse. 'Look, it's our friend,' she said and reached for the knocker.

'I'm not your friend,' said the knocker before she could knock. 'I've never even met yous.'

Julie jumped and let out a squeak.

'Beg your pardon,' said Aisling gravely. 'What my … companion here meant was that you resemble someone we spoke to recently.'

'Ah, that'll be The Lungs. Though he doesn't like it when we call him that.'

'Why not?' said Julie.

The merhorse-knocker laughed, a rattling, wheezy laugh that sounded like a handful of stones being tossed around in a metal bucket. 'Says it's not right to call a craythur by a derogatory make-name. And I says to him, "Sure, what's derogatory about that? And isn't it true, besides, that you've a pair of lungs on you to beat the band?" Sure, he's the only one out of the lot of them that can be in the River and talking to someone on the quays. That's how I knew who yous meant.'

'I see,' said Aisling. 'Well, perhaps you can help us, if you're free?'

'If I'm free? If I'm free, she says. I'm only a bleedin' door-knocker. What would I be doing if I wasn't free?'

'You make an excellent point,' said Aisling, 'but I didn't want to impose. Will you help us, then?'

'If I can,' said the knocker, 'but if yous want someone to carry your shopping, yous are out of luck.'

Aisling nodded, her face perfectly serious, and said, 'I'll bear that in mind.'

Julie turned away and bit the insides of her cheeks to keep from laughing.

'Really,' Aisling went on, 'all we wanted was to know – it's so quiet. There are no people around, apart from yourself, of course, and … em … "The Lungs". Is something going on? Where is everybody?'

The knocker was quiet for a long moment. Julie felt the suppressed laughter fading away and she turned to face the door. The knocker's expression hadn't changed much – perhaps it couldn't change much, being made of metal – but she thought it looked a little sterner than before.

'Yous are new,' it said at last. 'Blow-ins! I should have guessed before. Well, no help for it now. The gates are closed and yous are stuck here until they open again, and that won't be soon.'

'That's what The Lungs said,' said Julie. 'But why isn't there anyone on the streets?'

'Same reason the gates are closed,' said the knocker. 'Because the queen said so. There's a curfew, see? And yous are out well past it, so it's as well that the likes of me don't give a tinker's cuss what the queen says, or yous'd feel the long arm of the law on yer shoulders.'

'The law?' said Aisling. 'Would we be arrested?'

'Arrested! Sure, that's not the half of it. Yous'd be sent to the Tower and chained up until the queen said to let yous go.' The knocker sniffed, a lengthy and very wet-sounding sniff that made Julie want to blow her nose. 'This queen isn't like the Queen-that-was. She's a feckin' dragon if ever I saw one. Not a hair out of place, not a step out of line – all bite and no bark.'

Julie and Aisling exchanged a worried glance.

'Do you think we could come in, then?' said Julie. 'You wouldn't want us to get into trouble.'

The knocker gave them both a considering look. 'If it was up to me, I'd have yous warming yereselves by the fire as soon as look at yous, but I'm only the knocker, you understand? I'll do me best, but it's the head of the house that opens this door and it's she'll close it – whichever side yous are on when she does. You follow me?'

Julie and Aisling nodded.

'Well, as long as that's understood.' The knocker took a deep breath and lifted itself up into the air. 'Mind yeer ears!' it cried and banged itself down on the door once, twice, three times, louder than any doorknocker Julie had ever heard.

Before the clang of the third knock had died down, the little door that Julie had thought of as a giant peephole had opened, and a grumpy wrinkled face had appeared at it.

'What?' said the face.

'Forgive us for intruding,' said Aisling, 'but we're new to the City and we didn't realise there was a curfew. Would you be so kind as to shelter us so that we don't get in trouble?'

The face looked at her oddly. 'Did you swallow a dictionary or what? There's no call to be talking like a nob round these parts. You want to come in?'

'Um. Yes.'

'Can yous pay rent?'

'Eeeehm …'

Julie tugged at Aisling's coat-sleeve and whispered in her ear, 'Say yes, for God's sake!'

'But rent? Do you have enough money for that?'

'We only need to stay for one night. And anyway, the important thing is to get indoors before we get caught.'

'Good point.' Aisling smiled at the unsmiling face and said at a normal volume, 'Of course we can pay rent! No problem whatsoever!'

The face snorted. 'Well, yous might as well come in, then.'

The door to the peephole slammed shut and there was a tooth-clenching shriek and groan of metal scraping over metal, and then the door opened, revealing a dim entrance hall with a rush-strewn floor and a high cobwebby ceiling.

Julie swallowed at the sight of it. 'After you,' she said, nudging Aisling.

Aisling rolled her eyes and strode in as if it were her own front door, and Julie followed meekly after.

There was no sign of the person who'd opened the door to them, but Julie could hear a low buzz of conversation coming from somewhere near. Aisling opened the nearest door and peered around it.

'Staircase,' she said, closing it after her. 'Maybe this one –'

A wave of delicious warmth rushed out of the room as she opened the next door, and Julie shivered; she'd got so used to being cold that she'd forgotten what warm felt like. The room beyond the door looked like a kitchen – an ancient kitchen, with a huge stone chimney and a fire roaring in the hearth and a great big oak table in the middle of the floor. There was a shelf above the hearth that had pots and pans hanging from it, and a small television perched incongruously on the kitchen table. The ceiling and walls were painted white, but all the corners were grey with cobwebs.

A gruff voice said, 'Shut the door,' and Julie started and shut the door firmly behind her.

There were three men sitting by the hearth – two white and one black, all of them big and beefy looking. The black man was dressed in a dashiki and was sitting so close to the fire as to be almost on top of it, while the other two were further away, one of them (who had a greasy little moustache) reading a newspaper, and the other (who had heavy eyebrows and a low forehead) staring intently at the television, which seemed to be showing an episode of *Fair City*.

'Hello,' said Julie.

'Howaya,' said the man with the moustache, glancing up from his newspaper briefly. The heavy-browed man grunted and gave a little wave. The black man nodded distractedly, not looking away from the fire.

Aisling stood quite still, staring at the room and the three men. Julie rather liked the baffled look on her face. It wasn't a look she often wore in normal circumstances – not even in class, since she was one of those irritating people who always seemed to know everything about everything and got As without having to study.

Julie didn't know any more about their current situation than Aisling did, but Julie hadn't made a vocation out of knowing more than everyone around her, so it didn't bother her as much.

She walked up to the hearth and sat down beside the man with the moustache. 'Mind if I join you?' she said.

'Do as you like,' said the man, still not looking up from his paper. Julie tried to read as much of it as she could without drawing attention to herself. It didn't seem to be any of the papers she knew. It wasn't the *Metro Herald* or the *Evening Herald*; it wasn't the *Independent* or the *Times* or the *Examiner*, and it didn't look like a British paper either. She caught sight of a headline that read CURFEW EXTENDED TO DAYLIGHT HOURS – QUEEN 'ADAMANT', and when the man turned to a new page she saw another one that seemed to say THREE FINAL GATES TO MORTAL LANDS CLOSED. She was just on the verge of asking the man if she could read the paper when he was finished with it when he did finish and immediately tossed it into the fire.

'Same ould shite,' he muttered, spitting into the fire as it swallowed the paper, the blue flames licking along the front page and darkening the photograph of the grim-looking woman Julie took to be the queen.

The black man stirred, frowning. 'There is no need to use bad language, Jo Maxi,' he said.

'And you can go and shite yourself,' said Jo Maxi. 'There's every need when the gates are closed and the streets are empty. Even if we were let go out, there'd be no point, with no fares looking for a scooch. Isn't that right?' he said, turning to Julie.

'Em. Isn't what right?' she said.

'That the streets are empty. Not a soul to be seen.'

'Oh! Yes,' she said, wondering what a 'scooch' was, and why these three were so unsurprised that she and Aisling had come in, and so incurious about who they were. 'We just came from –'

'Ssh!' said the man with the eyebrows, lifting a finger to his mouth. 'Two minutes, please! Is nearly over!'

Jo Maxi and the black man exchanged long-suffering glances, and Julie looked up at the television. Now that she was up closer, she could see that the programme it was showing wasn't *Fair City* after all; it had the same kind of music and some of the actors looked familiar, but there was something different about it, though she couldn't put her finger on what until one of the characters drew a sword, kneeled down in front of another, and solemnly (and rather hammily) declared, 'I pledge myself to you, and only you!'

The end credits started rolling to the tune of the 'Marino Waltz', and the man with the eyebrows let out a long breath. 'Good episode,' he said to himself, then he looked around, seeming to notice where he was for the first time. 'Beg pardon,' he said to Julie, bowing slightly. He got up and turned the television off, and then bowed properly to her, and to Aisling, who was on the other side of the room, scrutinising the dresser. 'Very pleased to meet you. How may we call you?'

'I'm Julie,' said Julie, 'and this is my – this is Aisling.'

The man with the moustache stood up, nodding, and bowed to them both. ''Tis an honour, indeed. You can call me Jo Maxi. This telly addict here's called Prawo Jazdy. Mr Unpronounceable can introduce himself.'

The black man stood up, gave a bow that was by far the most graceful of the three, and said, 'You can call me Abayomiolorunkoje. That means "People wanted to humiliate me, but God would not let them".'

'I see,' said Julie, though she didn't; not really.

'I was rude, I know, but you must forgive,' said Prawo Jazdy, gesturing to the television. 'Is only programme about this city. Is not very good, but is all we have.'

'And he won't let us say a word while he's watching it,' said Jo Maxi, clapping Prawo Jazdy on the shoulder, 'not even to introduce ourselves to a guest. So don't think we're always like that. Now, is there anything we can do for yous?'

'Your name's not really Jo Maxi, is it?' said Aisling, as she sat down at the kitchen table.

The three men looked at each other with baffled expressions. 'Of course not,' said Jo Maxi. 'Sure, Aisling's not your real name either, is it?'

'Of course it –'

'What if it was?' said Julie, interrupting Aisling. 'Is there some problem with using real names?'

The three men still looked baffled. Abayomiolorunkoje was the first to recover.

'Names are powerful things,' he said. 'There is magic in names. Give someone your true name and you give them power over you. Only the very powerful and the very foolish give out their true names to anyone who asks.'

No prizes for guessing which category we're in, Julie thought grimly.

'Well, anyway,' said Aisling, smiling sweetly, 'maybe you can explain some things to us. We're new here, you see, and to be honest, we're finding this city a bit hard to understand.'

'You are not only ones!' said Prawo Jazdy, sitting down at the other end of the table. 'I've lived here five years now and I am still confused.'

Behind his back, Jo Maxi tapped his temple with a

knowing expression aimed at Aisling, which prompted a disapproving look from Abayomiolorunkoje. For a disconcerting second, Julie thought there was something odd about his eyes, the way they glittered and refracted the light, almost like a fly's eyes.

'What do yous want to know?' said Jo Maxi, sitting down next to Prawo Jazdy.

'Well …' said Julie slowly.

'The queen,' said Aisling. 'We've heard that she's closed the gates and brought in a curfew. Why?'

Abayomiolorunkoje looked around the room fearfully, then sat down at the table on Jo Maxi's other side. Julie thought that made it look like Aisling was being interviewed for a job or interrogated by the police, and she didn't like that, so she walked over to the other end of the table and sat down next to her. Aisling gave her a brief grateful look before leaning forward towards the men and saying, 'Well. Why? What's going on? Why is the city so quiet? Why is the queen shutting things down? Who is the queen, anyway?'

Jo Maxi took a deep breath. 'This place has always had three queens – three queens for three castles, you see? The Queen-that-was, the Queen-that-is and the Queen-that-will-be. They turn and turn about and every one of them gets a go at being the Queen-that-is. The Queen-that-is dies, you see, and becomes the Queen-that-was, and the Queen-that-will-be becomes the Queen-that-is, and the Queen-that-was comes back to life and becomes the Queen-that-will-be, all in a circle. Do you follow me?'

'Not really,' said Julie.

'The queen is dead, long live the queen?' said Aisling.

'Exactly,' said Jo Maxi. 'It was a trick they played on Death when they were one person, to keep the City in decent hands. Split one life into three and play pass-the-parcel with the crown. Only nowadays … well, they had a small little difference of opinion that ended in one of the queens running away, one of them taking the throne, and one of them being locked up. All three of them alive at the one time.' He shuddered visibly. 'It's not natural, so it's not! The Queen-that-was is hanging in a cage at the top of the Tower of Light, and there are worms crawling in her wounds and birds pecking at her flesh – but she can't die. The Queen-that-is won't *let* her die.'

'If she were to die, the cycle would begin,' said Abayomiolorunkoje. 'The Queen-that-is keeps her alive so that there will be no cycle any more, only one queen on the throne forever.'

'That's horrible!' said Julie.

'It is,' said Aisling, 'but it doesn't explain the curfew.'

'Will you let the priest say Mass?' said Jo Maxi, irritated. 'I was getting to that bit!'

'Sorry.'

'Chiselers today have no patience. 'N anyway, why

they fought they never said. Not to the likes of us.
But the gates were closed and the guards were raised
against invaders and spies, so that was probably it.'

'Invaders?' said Julie.

'Is a pretext,' said Prawo Jazdy. 'Is true the queen
fears invaders, but she also wishes for no one to take
the Queen-that-will-be out of the City. She wishes to
capture the Queen-that-will-be, to imprison her like
she imprisoned the Queen-that-was. That is why the
curfew –'

'Shh!' said Abayomiolorunkoje.

'Walls have ears, you sap!' said Jo Maxi.

'I was not going to say her name!'

'Don't even come close to saying it!' said
Abayomiolorunkoje. 'She can find those who talk
about her!'

'But I did not say her name! I am not stupid!'

'Who are you talking about?' said Aisling.

All three men turned to look at her, and Julie did
too, putting on her best pitying face. Aisling slapped
her forehead. 'Sorry. Stupid question. You can't talk
about her. OK.'

'Anyone the queen even thinks might be in league
with the invaders, or with the Queen-that-will-be, or
the Queen-that-was, or … your woman we can't talk
about … gets grabbed by the guards,' said Jo Maxi.
'The Tower's bursting with prisoners.'

'What about the Wormwood Gate?' said Julie. 'Is it

really the only way out of the City? And if it is, how can we find it?'

The three men exchanged more wary glances. 'Your woman would know,' said Jo Maxi. 'She's good at finding things.'

'She is also good at not being found,' said Abayomiolorunkoje. 'No one even knows what forms she can take.'

'There's one or two we know about – the dog and the butterfly –'

'But she has died at least eight times,' said Prawo Jazdy. 'So what are six other forms? Nobody knows. She could be one of seagulls guarding the Queen-that-was.'

'She wouldn't!' said Jo Maxi, scandalised. 'She'd never – she made a *promise*.'

Julie leaned over and murmured to Aisling, 'There was a horse when we came through the gate, wasn't there?'

Aisling nodded. 'I'd forgotten, but you're right. It knocked us over, and then here we were. Well, not here, but, you know. *Here*.'

The men stopped their argument and stared at them.

'What horse was this?' said Prawo Jazdy.

'It was white, wasn't it?' said Julie, still looking at Aisling, who nodded. 'With a red mane.'

The three men looked at each other in shock. 'White, with a red mane – and it came through the gate to mortal lands?' said Abayomiolorunkoje.

Julie tried to replay the scene in her mind. 'Well …' she said hesitantly.

'I think so,' said Aisling. 'Though we weren't really paying attention. It had just knocked us over.'

Jo Maxi's face fell. 'She can't. She wouldn't!'

'She could come back,' said Abayomiolorunkoje.

'But all the gates are closed,' said Prawo Jazdy.

'Except the Wormwood Gate,' said Aisling. 'And you said she was good at finding things.'

But Abayomiolorunkoje was shaking his head before she even finished the sentence. 'The Wormwood Gate cannot be seen from the other side,' he said. 'Even she … This is grave news,' he said, shaking his head sadly.

Jo nodded. 'No point being careful now,' he said. He took a handkerchief out of his trouser pocket and wiped his forehead with it, then blew his nose with a trumpeting sound. 'That horse was Molly Red, the Oathbreaker,' he said after he'd put the handkerchief away. 'She used to work for the Queen of Crows and the Lord of Shadows. Then she worked for the Queen-that-was, and now …'

'No,' said Prawo Jazdy, 'no, no, no! She would not do that! Not Molly Red!'

'She has only one life left,' said Jo Maxi, 'and she's using it to escape the City and go to mortal lands. What else can it mean? She's left us behind. Molly Red has left us behind.'

Prawo Jazdy and Abayomiolorunkoje exchanged glum looks. 'Then there is no hope,' said Prawo Jazdy.

'No hope for us to get home?' said Julie, her heart sinking.

'That too,' said Prawo Jazdy. 'But I meant that there is no hope for the City. Without Molly Red, there is no one who will stand against the queen.'

3

Aisling had always liked the idea of travelling to a magical world, but the prospect of being stuck in one was less enticing, even if she was stuck there with Julie, who was easily the most attractive girl in their year and very good company when she wasn't in a bitchy mood. (Really, if she was honest with herself, she enjoyed Julie's company even when she was in full-on hyperbitch mode, which was probably evidence of masochistic tendencies or unhealthy attachment patterns or something.)

She listened to the three men talking for as long as she could stand it, trying to make sense of the situation they were all in. The conversation had revolved around Molly Red and somebody called the Lord of Shadows whom they hated but were apparently obliged to be friendly to, and somebody called the Queen of Crows, who was definitely *not* the Queen of the City. (They had been positively offended at the question, which Aisling thought was a bit much. It seemed a reasonable thing to ask.) Her attention had wandered after her third futile attempt to get an explanation of who these people were and why they mattered. She could tell that all three of the men were pessimistic, Jo Maxi most of all, and that he in particular seemed to think that the City of the Three Castles had gone badly downhill lately and was doomed to destruction, but she got nowhere when she tried to figure out why he thought that. It was like watching a current-affairs programme in a foreign country: the general shape of what was happening seemed to make sense to the people talking, but none of the details meant anything to her.

So she had taken out her phone and started fiddling with it. There was no reception, of course (wherever they were – and she didn't even have a theory about that – they were miles away from the nearest Vodafone tower), but more puzzling was the fact that the camera wasn't working. She could see a preview image if she held the lens up to the thing she wanted to photograph, but no matter what she did with the settings none of the pictures she took seemed to record.

She wanted to point this out to Julie and get her to experiment with her own phone, but Julie was writing in her notebook. Aisling leaned over to read what she had written and saw:

'*CITY OF THE THREE CASTLES*
(city) (Realms Between [formerly Kingdom of Crows])'
and underneath that:
'*Ruled by three queens*'
but that was crossed out, and underneath it she had written:

'*Ruled by a queen. Formerly ruled by a triumvirate of three queens serving in rotation.*'

'It should be "triumfeminate",' Aisling murmured. '"Triumvirate" means "group of three men", from *tres* meaning "three" and *vir* meaning "man". You know, like in "virile".'

Julie scowled, closed the notebook, and slapped her on the arm with it. 'Nobody likes a hairsplitter,' she said. 'Anyway, do you have any ideas? We can't stay here forever.'

Aisling turned to the men. 'Excuse me,' she said, 'would you mind telling me what hours the curfew applies?'

'Sundown to sunup,' said Prawo Jazdy.

'Prime taxi hours,' said Jo Maxi mournfully. 'It's as if she's doing it to bankrupt me.'

'Then we should stay inside tonight, to avoid the guards,' said Aisling. 'The head of the house said we could.'

'I'm getting sleepy,' said Julie. 'Do you … are there, like, spare rooms? Or a sofa or something?'

Abayomiolorunkoje stood up. 'Forgive our rudeness. Of course you must be tired. I will show you to the spare rooms.'

He picked up two candlesticks and lit the candles from the fire, then indicated with a jerk of his head that they should follow him. Aisling went first, looking around the kitchen as she left to fix its image in her mind. It wasn't what she'd imagined a kitchen in a magical land would look like, and that seemed important, somehow, because it meant it was more likely to be real. She would never have dreamed up anything as unremarkable as this.

Her room was dark and old-fashioned, with a four-poster bed and a huge chest of drawers in old mahogany. She took one of the candlesticks from Abayomiolorunkoje with a smile and a nod, and he nodded back and wished her a good night before escorting Julie to a different room.

Aisling set the candlestick on the bedside table and flopped down on the bed, lying the wrong way across it, on top of the covers. She was much too excited to sleep, but she was glad of the excuse to be alone. She did her best thinking alone.

Merhorses. Three massive fires. Jo Maxi and Prawo Jazdy. It was all familiar, though some of it was so distantly familiar that she wasn't sure she'd ever figure out where she'd heard or seen it before. It was plain to her that the City of the Three Castles was a half-place,

57

a between-place, the kind of place she would describe as 'liminal' if she thought anyone would understand what she meant. It wasn't quite real in its own right. It was made out of images and fragmentary memories, and there was no way of knowing what logic it was ruled by. Dream logic, probably, the kind of logic where a gate could be visible on one side only, and a queen could be three people and one person at the same time, and a woman could turn into a horse.

She stood up abruptly, grabbed the candlestick and strode out of the room. She needed – *they* needed– a lot more information if they were going to find a way back to Dublin without being turned into squid because they mispronounced somebody's name.

At the door of the kitchen, she hesitated. She could hear the men talking, their voices raised in – excitement? Anger? She pinched the candleflame to snuff it and leaned in, listening carefully.

'... the game's worth the candle, but only if we get them both,' Jo Maxi was saying.

'We will have to wait for dawn and curfew's end,' said Prawo Jazdy. 'No use to bring intruders to the Tower if the guards will arrest us for breaking curfew.'

'I am not sure about this,' said Abayomiolorunkoje. 'Is this really a good idea?'

'What else can we do?' said Jo Maxi, and there was a silence that seemed to weigh on them all, like the air pressure before a storm. Aisling held her breath.

'Will it save us?' Abayomiolorunkoje said quietly.

'It'll prove our loyalty to the queen,' said Jo Maxi. 'We can name our own reward – we can ask for a gate to be opened just long enough that we can leave.'

'Abandon the City?' said Prawo Jazdy.

'Don't be getting all sentimental on me, now. Sure, you're not even from here!'

'Jo Maxi is right,' said Abayomiolorunkoje. 'The City will not last long if the queen does not fall, and now that Molly Red has gone, there is not much hope that she will. It is best to escape while we can.'

'Then we are agreed,' said Prawo Jazdy. 'We wait until dawn, and then we take the mortal girls to the Tower of Light.'

That was all Aisling needed to hear. Heart pounding, she inched away from the door, moving as slowly and gradually as possible so that her boots wouldn't creak and give her position away. She inched her way up the stairs too, for they were made of old wood and creaked even more than her boots.

When she got to Julie's room, she opened the door quietly, and when she saw the candle still lit and Julie sitting up in bed, she raised a finger to her lips and said, 'Sh!' and crept over towards her.

'What are you doing here?' Julie whispered.

'Put your shoes on,' Aisling replied, also whispering. 'We have to get out of here. I overheard those three guys talking about what they should do about us.

Apparently there's a bounty available for anyone who brings intruders to the queen. They're going to hand us over and collect the reward.'

Julie blinked and rubbed her forehead. 'But they seemed so nice.'

'Yeah, well … nice is different than good,' Aisling said. 'Anyway, it doesn't matter. We have to leave before dawn or they'll take us to the queen, and then we'll be trapped for real.'

'All right. Give me a second.'

Aisling nodded and looked around the room while Julie put her shoes on and tied back her hair. Aisling wasn't sure she wanted to risk going down the stairs, past the door of the kitchen where the men were probably still planning how best to kidnap the two of them. She sized up the window. If the sash worked properly, it should be big enough.

She shoved it upwards. It rose smoothly and stayed open. 'Perfect,' she said to herself and gestured welcomingly to Julie. 'After you.'

Julie gave her a baleful look but stuck her head out the window anyway. 'How far down is it, do you think?'

Aisling stuck her head out beside Julie's and looked down. The windowsill was wide and sturdy, and the wall was well-supplied with drainpipes and Virginia creeper. Getting down would be easy.

Easy means predictable, said a little voice in her head. *Predictable means easily caught.*

'We're not going down,' she said. 'We're going up.'

Julie looked at her like she'd grown a second head. 'What are you talking about?'

'It's dry out, and pretty warm too, so we don't need to shelter from the weather, but we do need to shelter from the queen's guards. Don't you reckon we'll be better hidden on the roof than on the ground?'

Julie smiled, and Aisling felt her stomach wobble.

'Lateral thinking,' said Julie. 'I like it! But will you be able to climb with those boots of yours?'

'I hadn't thought of that. Do you think you can carry them over your shoulder, if I knot the laces together?'

'They're huge … I suppose so. Take them off, then.'

Now it was Aisling's turn to fiddle with her footwear. While Julie waited, she bounced up and down or back and forth on her feet, humming or singing to herself as if she had too much energy to stay still. She had always been like that, as long as Aisling had known her.

When the laces and buckles and Velcro were all undone, Aisling handed the boots over to Julie, who tied the laces together in a strong knot and balanced them over her right shoulder with all the care of a milkmaid balancing a pail on a yoke.

'Well,' Julie said, 'here goes nothing,' and she climbed out onto the windowsill and started ascending the wall.

She made it look … not easy, exactly, but doable, not much harder than vaulting the fence of Stephen's Green, which Aisling had done more than once. Aisling considered calling out to her to say 'I'm watching out for you' or 'Are you OK?', but thought better of it. Best not to break her concentration. It was a long way down to the street below, and Aisling wasn't sure she'd be able to catch Julie if she fell.

Julie made it to the sill of the window above, and there she stopped. 'Come up now,' she said, a little breathless. 'It's easy.'

'Easy for you,' Aisling muttered, too low for Julie to hear, then called up, 'All right.'

She set her hands on the farthest edge of the windowsill and half-climbed, half-pulled herself out onto it, perching on the sill and steadying herself with both hands leaning on the windowpane. Looking up, she tried to remember what Julie had done, tried to picture herself doing it, made compensations and adjustments in her head (she was bigger than Julie and wearing socks and a long coat). When she noticed Julie shuffling impatiently on the sill above, she realised she was overthinking it and stood straight up, reaching for the top edge of the window with one hand and a nearby drainpipe with another, and dragging herself up to a big clump of creeper that looked old enough and thick enough to carry her weight.

Once she'd pulled her feet off the sill, she heard

Julie calling to her in a low voice, 'Are you OK?'

'Fine,' she called back quietly, but not so quietly that Julie wouldn't hear her. 'Let me concentrate. I'm not good at this kind of thing.'

'Fair enough,' Julie replied, and then there was a silence which gave Aisling time to stare at the creeper, seeking out the places where the tendrils forked and combined, where they looked solidly connected to the wall. Slowly but surely, she made her way up, seeking out two new footholds before she moved to the next: a hole in the brickwork here, a brace on the wall there, and then the windowsill on the floor above Julie's bedroom. Carefully, carefully, she inched her way sideways, her heart quivering and thumping every time she shifted her hand from one hold to a new one. Finally, she put one foot on the windowsill, then the other, and she was at last able to crouch down and take a deep breath.

'You make this look so easy,' she panted, and she had meant it as a compliment, but it came out sounding like an accusation. *I keep doing that*, she thought with some irritation, *and it is not helping*.

But Julie smiled. 'There are so many jokes I could make right now, but I'm going to be the better person and not make any of them. Aren't you grateful?'

'Yes. Yes, my heart is overflowing.'

Julie chuckled. 'I'm going up. One more storey and we're on the roof, and then we can – GAH!'

Aisling shrieked at the same time as Julie, for the window behind them had opened. Aisling twisted her neck round, her heart pounding in her throat, and exhaled sharply when she saw who it was: not one of the three men, but the wizened old face (she couldn't tell if it was male or female) that had opened the door for them.

She shifted around to face it properly and her stomach lurched: it was just a face, or perhaps a head, with a shock of white hair with one red streak, floating in the air with no body attached. 'What are yous two up to?' said the face.

'Um,' said Julie, her face completely blank.

'Er,' said Aisling, her mind racing to come up with an excuse.

'Are yous trying to get out of paying the rent?' the face went on, 'because I wouldn't advise that. No, I wouldn't advise that at all.'

'We're not –'

'Rent?' said Aisling. 'We haven't even been here a whole night! I hardly think you can charge us rent for that.'

'When you have a house with a lock on the door, you can charge me rent when I come and visit,' said the face, 'but this is my house, and it runs by my rules.'

'Charming,' muttered Aisling. She looked at Julie and shrugged, mouthing, *Any ideas?*

'What kind of rent do you want us to pay?' said Julie. 'We have to get out of here quickly.'

The face eyed them both. 'Would yous be on the run from the guards, by any chance?'

Julie glanced at Aisling, and Aisling nodded. 'You could say that,' she said. 'We're not from here, and we don't really understand what's going on, but we don't want to be locked away.'

The face grinned, which was a most uncanny sight: all of the wrinkles rearranged themselves in a different pattern, and the eyes grew bright and almost mischievous. 'Foreigners!' it said, chuckling. 'Doesn't that beat the band? Well, then, in that case you can pay your rent now: swear an oath to me that you'll leave the City with a better ruler than it had when you came here.'

Aisling and Julie exchanged dubious looks. 'I'm not sure that's the kind of thing we can *promise* to do,' Aisling began. 'I mean, with the best will in the world, humanitarian interventions have a way of backfiring.'

'Yeah,' said Julie, 'and it's not like we know who'd be the best ruler for this place. We're not even from here.'

'There's things a foreigner can do in the City that none of us that are from here can do. And yous don't need to promise to give the City the best ruler it can have. Only to leave it with a better one than it has now.'

'What do you think?' Julie murmured.

Aisling glanced around, avoiding looking straight down. 'I don't think we have a choice, frankly. And this isn't a promise to actually do anything, so I think we'll be all right.'

'Don't have a choice? It's a floating head. What can it do to us?'

'It's a *disembodied head* that is *floating in mid-air*. What *can't* it do?'

'Good point.' Julie turned back to the head. 'So, we have to promise to –'

'Leave the City of the Three Castles with a better ruler than it had when yous came.'

'Fair enough,' said Julie, raising her right hand as if she were in court. 'I swear that I will leave the City of the Three Castles with a better ruler than it had when I arrived.' She nudged Aisling to do the same, and Aisling repeated the words. As she said them, she felt a strange tightness settle down over her head, and then over the rest of her body. It vanished as suddenly as it had come, but she had an uneasy feeling that she had done more than say some words and raise her hand.

'That's that sorted,' said the face. 'Good night, so. And good luck.' The window closed, somehow, and the curtains closed behind it, leaving the two of them alone on the windowsill.

'Well,' said Aisling, 'that was strange.'

'Oh,' said Julie, '"head of the house". I get it now.'

Aisling laughed. 'Me too! God, that's awful. Is this place run on puns or something?'

Julie grimaced. 'I hope not. Like something out of a Piers Anthony novel.'

'You've read Piers Anthony?'

'Yes. Why, have you?'

'Well … no. I'm just surprised that you have.'

'You don't actually know me that well,' said Julie, a note of bitterness in her voice that gave Aisling a strange pang. 'Anyway,' she said briskly, 'let's get going.'

The rest of their climb was conducted in a silence punctuated only by grunts and pants and the occasional muttered swearword. When they got to the roof, Julie lay back against the sloping slate tiles and stared up at the sky. Aisling sat down beside her. From here, she could see the stars, and they looked different; she tried to pick out constellations, but she couldn't see them – not even Orion, which was always the easiest to see when it was in season. The stars seemed to have been sprinkled randomly on the sky, like hundreds-and-thousands on a cake. They were thickly and evenly spread – much more so than in the night sky she was used to – but they didn't seem to form any patterns. Nothing to navigate by, even for a migrating bird.

A discouraging thought occurred to her.

'It's just struck me,' she said, panting, 'if it turns out that the queen's guards *can* fly, this whole exercise will have been a wasted effort.'

Julie slapped Aisling's arm half-heartedly. 'Don't be so negative! We'll never get back with that kind of attitude.'

'I'm just pointing out possibilities. Give me my boots back.'

Julie handed her the boots, and Aisling set to untangling the laces.

'Were you a Girl Guide or something, Julie? This knot is ridiculous.'

'My dad sails,' said Julie. 'He taught me how to tie knots when I was a kid. Proper knots that won't come undone with a tug.'

'I wish this one *would* come undone with a tug. Or that I'd brought that candle up with me.'

'Don't be stupid. How could you climb with a candlestick in your hand?'

'How can I untie this knot when I can barely see the laces? Wait – hold on a second – aha! Victory is mine!'

The knot came undone and the boots fell to the roof with a thump.

'Those things are so complicated,' said Julie as Aisling was putting them back on. 'I don't know why you bother with them.'

'And I suppose your hair just looks like that when you get out of bed in the morning, and your eyelids are naturally purple?'

'Point.' Julie rolled over on her side, which looked uncomfortable. 'But why go to so much effort to look weird? Do you like people staring at you?'

'Depending on who I'm hanging out with, I can be the most normal person in the room.'

'I doubt that.'

'I know a guy who had his tongue split.'

Julie sat bolt upright. 'Seriously?' She looked like she was about to vomit.

Aisling laughed. 'No, but I know somebody who knows a guy who had his tongue split. I promise you, I may be the weirdest person you know, but I am not the weirdest person I know. Not by a long shot.'

'I was right, then.'

'About what?'

'You *do* dress like that to fit in with your spookykid mates.'

Aisling could feel her cheeks warming up. 'Maybe,' she muttered. 'I mean, that's not all there is to it, but yeah, that's part of it.'

There was a silence, and Aisling was grateful for the buckles and Velcro on her boots that gave her something to do with her hands, an excuse for not talking.

'I'm not sure about these leggings,' said Julie, the words coming out in a rush. 'I mean, like you said, they were Tina's idea. I'm not really … they're not really … I'm not sure about them.'

'Nah, they look good on you,' said Aisling. *You look good in them*, she thought, *but you look good in everything.*

There was a high, eerie cry from overhead. They both looked up to see a flock of seagulls swooping and turning in the sky.

'I don't want to stay in one place for too long,' said Julie. 'You might be right about the queen's guards. Maybe they *can* fly. Anyway, these slates aren't very comfortable.'

Aisling sighed, but pulled herself all the way upright. 'All go around here, isn't it? Come on, let's go this way.' She scrambled up the slope of the roof and down to the valley between the roof's two peaks, Julie following. 'This way,' she said, 'we won't be visible from the street. At least, I don't think we will.'

The valley was too narrow to walk in, and the only way to make progress at all was to have one foot on the right-hand slope and one on the left-hand slope, which was tricky in thick-soled boots.

Even Julie, in her ballet flats, was having trouble with it. 'This is awkward,' she muttered.

'Yeah, a bit,' said Aisling, 'but I'd rather go this way than try walking along the peaks, wouldn't you? Or the outside slopes. You could fall all the way down to the street.'

Julie shuddered. 'Oh, don't!' She stopped walking.

'What is it?' said Aisling.

'They called us "mortals". What do you think that means?'

Aisling shrugged. 'By a process of elimination, if

we're mortals and they're not, they must be immortals of some kind, I suppose. Probably not like in *Highlander*, but –'

'But not dying. Or coming back after they die. They said that the queen … when one queen dies, another one takes her place, and then – did you follow that?'

'They go round in a circle. The Queen-that-was, the Queen-that-is, the Queen-that-will-be. Taking turns to be alive, by the sound of it.'

'And they said about your woman, Molly Red, that she'd died before. So it sounds like the people here do die, and when they do, they come back.'

Aisling considered this. 'Instant reincarnation. Interesting. That would explain what they said about Molly Red having different forms. Maybe each time you die here, you come back in a different form.'

'Well, maybe, but does that apply to us?'

Aisling looked at her, startled. 'No,' she said slowly, 'probably not. Though, really, who knows? But … no, I wouldn't think so.'

'No, me neither.' Julie gave her a nudge, and they started walking again. 'So we should be careful,' she said after a while, 'because … because this isn't a dream.'

'No,' said Aisling. 'No, it's not.'

It was a weighty thought, and she was so busy digesting it that she had to stop one step before the end of the roof, so abruptly that Julie bumped into her and clutched at her arms to keep from falling.

'Watch it! What're you stopping for?'

'I ran out of roof,' said Aisling. 'You did say we should be careful.'

'Oh. That's, um …'

Aisling sighed. 'Yeah.' She squatted down, squashed uncomfortably between the two slopes of the roof. 'I have to admit that, um … that I didn't completely think this through,' she said in a rush. 'I mean, I still think it was a good idea to get away from those three guys, and to go on the roof rather than the ground, but as to what would happen when we were up here … I sort of hoped it would be possible to improvise.'

'Improvise what? A helicopter?'

Aisling glared at her. 'If you have any ideas on how to improve our situation, I'm open to suggestions.'

'Is there a fire escape?'

'Where do you think we are, New York? No, there isn't a fire escape.'

'A drainpipe, then. Or a window ledge? We climbed up. There must be a way to climb down.'

'Stand back a bit and I'll look.'

Julie scuttled back crabwise, and Aisling crouched down and shifted her body back so that she could lie face-down in the valley and peer over the side of the roof. The wall was a plain gable-end, with no windows, no creeper, no drainpipes within reach, not even a bit of uneven brickwork to grab onto. She pushed herself back up into a sitting position and shook her head.

'Nothing?' said Julie.

'Nothing.'

Julie looked despondent, and then she started laughing.

'What?' said Aisling.

'I just realised … even though I'm trapped on the roof of a building with no phone service and no way of getting down, this is actually the most fun I've had in months.'

Aisling grinned, warmth rising in her cheeks and her belly. 'Yeah,' she said, 'me too,' and then, because that felt like giving away too much, she stood up and spread her arms. 'Look at the view!'

From their vantage point on the roof, Aisling could see a ribbon of river snaking through the mostly-dark city, the darkness punctuated by many small white lights and three big red ones – the fires: the three burning castles. The city grew misty beyond the areas illuminated by the fires; there was a vague suggestion of mountains in one direction, something that might have been a bay in another, a wide strip that was probably a road stretching out towards a third.

Julie stood up beside her and looked. 'Yeah,' she said. 'It's amazing. Makes me wish my camera was working.'

'Yours isn't working either?'

'Nope. What do you think that's about?'

'I don't know,' said Aisling, frowning. She took out her phone and fiddled with it a little, then put it back in her pocket. 'I mean, I have a theory.'

'Well, let's hear it, then.'

'Well ... Well, it's totally speculative and not exactly grounded in anything other than the observations I've been able to make since we arrived here, and it might be complete nonsense and disproved by the next thing we see, and in any case I'm not completely –'

'Aisling!'

'Right. Yes. Em. Well, you know what I said earlier, about this being a hallucination? What if it sort of is, only –'

There was a shriek and a cry from overhead. She broke off. There was another cry, then another, then a chorus of shrieks all at once, and a flock of seagulls descended to swoop around them in a circle. Julie ducked down into a crouch, and Aisling followed a second later, sweeping her arm around Julie to cover her with her coat and peering up at the birds. There were dozens of them, squealing and lamenting like lost souls, wheeling around and around so fast that the wind from their wings made her eyes water.

'This isn't normal!' Aisling said, shouting to be heard over the gulls' cries. 'Seagulls don't act like this!'

'I don't think they are seagulls,' Julie shouted back. 'I think they're –'

Whatever she thought they were, Aisling never

heard it, because the gulls chose that moment to swoop in and grab hold of her by the epaulettes and belt of her coat. Aisling cried out and let go of Julie, but Julie grabbed Aisling's lapels and clung on for all she was worth.

'Let go!' Aisling cried, a little less loudly, now that some of the gulls' beaks were occupied. 'They won't be able to grab you –'

'I'm not letting them take you!' Julie shouted. 'They won't be able to carry us both!'

'Don't be stupid! Let go!' Aisling tried to prise Julie's hands from her coat, but the gulls grabbed onto her sleeves. They grabbed Julie's belt as well, and the hems of her leggings, and the straps of her bra. Aisling saw tears rising in Julie's eyes as the gulls' beaks pecked at her skin.

'It's too late anyway,' said Julie, grabbing Aisling around the waist and ducking her head.

The gulls flapped their wings, and then the girls were lifted from the roof with a sickening lurch, and there was nothing beneath their feet any more. For a moment Aisling panicked, kicking out as if that would do any good. Julie squirmed too, but the gulls only flapped all the harder. Then Aisling felt Julie's left foot touching the toe of her right boot, and her right foot touching the toe of her left boot. *Like a little girl dancing with her father*, she thought, and then, *but there's no dance floor. There's no floor. There's just –*

'Hey,' said Julie, 'it's going to be all right.'

Aisling could feel a sob building up in her throat. She bit her lip to keep from crying.

'Listen,' said Julie, her voice perfectly even, 'now's not a good time to break down, OK? They're going to have to set us down some time, and when they do that you can cry as much as you like. But right now you need to take a deep breath and stay calm. Can you do that?'

Aisling stared at her, her mind blank.

'Come on,' Julie said. 'Inhale. Deep breath. Let your belly expand. Can you do that?'

Aisling closed her eyes and breathed in.

'OK, now exhale for a count of four, but preferably not in my face because I don't know what you've been eating.'

Aisling scowled and exhaled pointedly in Julie's face.

'There, see?' said Julie, laughing a little. 'Now you're yourself again.'

'You know, it's *remarkable* how you manage to be a bitch even when you're trying to be nice.'

'I've been with you all night,' said Julie. 'I've been taking notes.'

'If I had a free hand, I'd slap you.'

'I stopped you crying, didn't I?'

Aisling opened her mouth to speak, but before she could say anything there was a flurry and a bump and they were dropped unceremoniously to the ground. The seagulls circled around them once, crying out all the while, and then flew away in a burst of white feathers.

Julie rolled off Aisling and Aisling scrambled to her feet. They were surrounded by men in strange, old-fashioned uniforms and helmets with face-guards, carrying halberds. The halberds were lowered, with the spiky bits aimed at the two of them.

'You are under arrest, by orders of the queen,' said one of the men, whose uniform bore a red sash across his chest, 'for trespassing, violation of curfew, climbing on a roof without a licence and intent to commit regicide.'

Julie raised her hands in protest. 'Hey, what? Regicide? We don't want to kill the queen!'

The man with the red sash sniffed. 'Pfft, that's what they all say. Haul 'em in, lads!'

The guards seemed only too eager to do as he said – so eager, in fact, that both Aisling and Julie were grabbed by four guards each, two for each arm. It made their progress rather slow as they were marched from their landing spot to a narrow iron gate where yet another guard was waiting. This one wasn't wearing a helmet; Aisling was somehow not surprised to see that he had the head of a dog, though it did make her wonder what the other guards were hiding.

'Another pair?' he said listlessly. 'All right, then.

Make sure you do the paperwork; I'm not doing it for you.'

He swung the gate open, and there was a bit of a scuffle as the guards holding on to Aisling and Julie silently competed over which was going to have the privilege of holding on to them while they were passing through the gate. The scuffle sorted itself out (after the chief guard gave the others some meaningful looks), and the two girls were frogmarched through the gate, down a narrow stone corridor, down a short flight of stairs and into a small cell with a wooden door.

'You'll be staying here at Her Majesty's pleasure,' said the chief guard with a sneer in his voice. 'Don't expect a quick trial. Or any trial, if she doesn't feel like giving you one.'

He slammed the door, and Aisling could hear a deadbolt being shot home and the clatter of hobnailed boots on stone receding into the distance.

'Well,' she said, once the sounds had died away, 'I have to admit that I am not remotely comforted by the fact that I foresaw this as a possibility.'

Julie stared at her. 'You're *weird*,' she said, turning to examine the cell.

It was small – not really big enough for both of them if they were going to be sleeping there; it had one bed, or rather a bench wide enough to serve as a bed if you didn't mind sleeping on bare wood. There was straw on the floor and an empty chamberpot in one corner.

It smelled clean, thankfully, and there was a window high up in the wall that looked out at ground level, but it wasn't big enough to climb through.

Aisling climbed up on the bench to peer through the window. There was light coming through it, and not just the light of the fires. 'It's almost morning,' she said.

'I don't feel tired,' said Julie, sitting down on the bench beside her. 'Isn't that strange?'

'Adrenaline, maybe? In which case we'll probably get the shakes in about an hour, unless something else happens.'

'No, I don't think that's it.' Julie took out her phone and stared at it. 'You know the way our cameras aren't working? Well, the clock isn't working either. Not on mine, anyway.'

'Huh.' Aisling took out her phone and looked at the clock display. She hadn't registered the time when she'd been fiddling with it before, but now that she was actually looking at it, she could see that something was wrong; there was no way it was only 9.13 p.m.

She stared and stared at it, waiting for the minute figure to tick over to 14, but though she counted to a hundred in her head, it never did.

'This just confirms my theory,' she said. 'Or at least, it's evidence in its favour.'

'You never said what your theory was.'

'Oh. Right. Well. This place is pretty obviously

based on Dublin, right? Or, it's like Dublin.'

'City of the Three Castles,' said Julie, taking her notebook out of her bag. 'Here, look –' She opened the notebook to a page with a sketch on it: three stylised castles, all aflame, and writing in Latin underneath it. 'This is the official crest of the City of Dublin.'

'Yes. Yes, exactly! So this is like … like a dream of Dublin. Or, a collective hallucination. You know? Like, I just remembered where I saw merhorses before – they're on the lampposts in the centre of town.'

'Cool.' Julie ran her fingers over the sketch and frowned. 'But what does that have to do with our phones not working?'

'Well, if this place isn't really *real*, it stands to reason we won't be able to take pictures of it. And time probably doesn't work normally here. So our phones are tracking time perfectly, just … they're tracking time in the real world, not here.'

'So when we get back, no time will have passed? Like the Pevensies coming back from Narnia?'

'Yes, exactly.' Aisling blinked, surprised. 'Wait, you've read the Narnia books?'

Julie rolled her eyes. 'Everyone's read the Narnia books. Stop assuming I can't read just because I listen to Top 40 hits.'

'Right. Sorry. Stereotyping, bad habit, won't do it again.'

'Yeah, don't.'

There was a pause, and Aisling thought that perhaps it ought to have been awkward, between one thing and another, but it wasn't. It was pleasant, comfortable; almost as if they were friends.

'You do Latin, don't you?' said Julie, breaking the silence.

'Yep. Why?'

'What does this mean?'

She held out the notebook, her finger pointing to the slogan underneath the crest.

'*Obedientia civium urbis felicitas*,' Aisling read. 'That's the motto of the city, I suppose?'

'Obviously. But what does it mean?'

'Um … "The obedience of the citizens is the happiness of the city"? Something like that.'

Julie looked around at the cell they were in and shivered visibly. 'Creepy,' she said.

'I know,' said Aisling. 'I know.'

Julie was trying to figure out what their next move should be when there was a high-pitched whining sound, as of metal scraping against metal, and the door of their cell slammed open. Julie leapt to her feet and Aisling followed suit. A guard walked in, not wearing his helmet, this one having the head of a horse. He looked at the two of them, turning his head to look now at Julie, now at Aisling, then nodded and grabbed Julie by the arm.

'Queen wants to see you,' he said. 'Come with me.'

'Wait, what?' said Julie, trying to pull her arm free.

'Why just her?' said Aisling. 'Why not both of us?'

'Could be you, but I'm not sure I could carry you up all them steps,' said the guard in a sniffy sort of way.

Aisling narrowed her eyes. 'Was that a crack about my weight?'

'Yes,' said the guard, not looking at her. 'Stop struggling,' he said to Julie. 'You're lucky to get to see the queen at all. You haven't even been in for a day yet. Some people have been waiting here for months for a hearing.'

Julie looked at Aisling, trying to communicate with her eyes that she thought it would be better to go along with this than to fight. Aisling seemed to get the point; she stepped back and sat back down on the bench. 'Nothing wrong with my weight,' she muttered to herself. 'I'm the perfect weight for who I am.'

Julie stopped resisting the guard's pull on her arm and let him drag her out to the corridor, where he slammed the door shut again and pushed the bolt home. He let go of her arm and made as if to grab her around the waist, but she skipped back a step and raised her hands.

'Look, do you have to carry me? I have legs, you know. I can walk.'

'Procedure,' said the guard. 'If I didn't carry you, I couldn't trust you not to run away, and that'd be a pain in the arse. Not that you could get away, because you'd get caught, but we'd have to chase you, and on the graveyard shift we try to avoid running around.'

'Well, couldn't you just give me a piggyback? I don't want to be hauled around like a sack of potatoes. It's not dignified.'

The guard shrugged and turned around, crouching

down. For a second, Julie contemplated running away while his back was turned, but she had no idea where the nearest exit was, and there were enough guards hanging around to make escape a very iffy proposition. She straddled his back instead and put her arms around his thick horse's neck. He stood up, lifting her, and started to jog along the corridor.

'Are there a lot of prisoners?' she asked as he reached a spiral staircase and started trotting up the steps. 'I heard that a lot of people are breaking curfew.'

The guard snorted a very loud, horsey snort. 'Stupid bleedin' law,' he muttered. 'Only makes work for us. And for what? The queen's already got everyone so terrified they can't sneeze unless she says so.'

'I see.' Julie thought back to the conversation the three men had had in the kitchen of the house. 'But aren't there, you know, rebels?'

The guard stopped on the stair. 'Rebels?'

'People who fight the queen. There must be!'

The guard hesitated, then turned his head and leaned his neck back so that she got a whiff of his breath (which smelled of porridge oats). 'That's dangerous talk, little miss,' he said quietly. 'You and I could both get into a lot of trouble just for mentioning it.'

Julie felt her heart speeding up. 'I'm already in as much trouble as I can be!' she said. 'I'm not afraid.'

'Well, I am,' said the guard, and he turned back around and went on trotting up the stairs.

Julie sagged down against his back. The most important thing was to get home, but she and Aisling had sworn an oath. Even if they found a way out of the City, they were duty-bound not to leave with the queen still on the throne. And that was an enormous 'if'.

They reached the top of the staircase, and the guard contemplated the door in front of them for a few seconds before raising his foot (which, Julie could see now, was actually a hoof with a metal shoe) and kicking it three times. 'Doesn't open from this side,' he said. 'Got to knock.'

'What if nobody's in?'

'Then you don't get to go in there. But there's always somebody there.'

There was a series of clattering and clicking noises, as of keys being turned or bolts being drawn, and the door was opened a few inches, enough to reveal the face of a guard – human this time – who glared at them suspiciously. 'What's the story?' said the guard.

'Mortal prisoner,' said the horse-head guard, tilting his head sideways to make it easier for the other guard to see Julie. 'There was two of them. Queen wanted to see one.'

'All right.' The door opened fully, and the horse-head guard trotted through it and down a short corridor that ended with a pair of vast double doors guarded by two helmeted men. The guards opened the doors without a word, and the horse-head guard trotted towards them, hesitated for a moment at the threshold, then passed into the room beyond.

It was a big room, a grand room, decorated in a style that Julie hadn't expected to see: blond pine, white carpet, geometrical furniture in solid colours, and floor-to-ceiling plate-glass windows looking out over the City. The rest of the City was so old-fashioned that Julie had taken for granted that the queen's chambers would be as well, but it looked like it had been furnished from an Ikea catalogue. It was a little unnerving.

'Set her down,' said a voice. It was a woman's voice, presumably the queen's, but Julie couldn't tell where it was coming from. The horse-head guard crouched down and let go of Julie's legs, and she stepped back, hopping from foot to foot to banish the pins and needles.

A very fancy-looking black leather office chair swivelled on its stand, and there she was: undoubtedly the queen. Here in this chamber, she could hardly be anyone else, but Julie thought she would have known her for an important person anywhere. She was dressed like an executive from an American movie, the kind who would make her company successful by firing employees for the slightest infraction but would turn out to have a hollow and lonely personal life (and probably end up falling in love with a waiter and retiring to have babies). Her hair was short and slicked back with something that made it glisten in the light, and her one visible eye was a hard and penetrating blue. The other eye was covered by a leather patch, which should have looked ridiculous with the dark suit and manicured nails, but somehow just added to her aura of power.

The guard fell to one knee and bowed his head. 'Your Majesty, the prisoner,' he said.

'Yes, yes, I see that. Watch the door from this side, but don't go just yet,' said the queen with a gesture of dismissal.

Julie stared as the guard bowed deeply and walked backwards towards the door. Weren't there countries where you weren't supposed to turn your back on the king or queen? A stupid rule, but the guard seemed used enough to it that he didn't bump into anything.

'So,' said the queen. Julie started and turned to face her, a blush spreading over her cheeks.

The queen smirked and stood up, striding over to a window and staring out of it, her hands clasped behind her back.

'I know who sent you,' she said, 'and I know what you're here to do. It won't happen, do you understand? I won't allow it to happen. The City is mine and will always be mine. I won it by fair combat and I will not lose it, by fair means or foul.'

'I don't know what you're talking about,' said Julie.

The queen laughed, a dry, mirthless sound. 'A pro-testation of innocence. How charming! How utterly charming! You've come this far and been found out, and you still think you can bluff your way past me.' She turned her head so that her face was in profile, her one good eye fixed on Julie. 'Although from another point of view, that might be considered insulting.'

'I'm not bluffing,' said Julie. 'I didn't mean to do anything when I came here. I came here by accident, and all I want to do is go home.'

The queen pivoted round to face her in a move so smooth and sharp that Julie suspected she had practised it for hours. 'Do you take me for a fool?' she growled. 'The Lord of Shadows has ignored my message and sent no aid against the Queen of Crows. Thus I know: he plans to break the treaty with my death and the deaths of my sister-queens! I know too that he is a lying mortal! I know he is the consort of the Queen of Crows! I know Molly Red is his servant! All this I know, mortal, so you betray nothing if you admit this much.'

'I honestly have no idea what you're talking about,' said Julie. 'I mean, who are these people? The Queen of Crows? The Lord of Shadows? The names are sort of familiar, but that's all. And I've heard a bit about Molly Red, but I've never met her.' As soon as she finished the sentence, it occurred to her that that last part wasn't entirely true, though it was true enough.

She was pretty sure being run over by a horse didn't really count as *meeting* the horse.

'Pfah! Do you expect me to believe that when Molly Red opened the Wormwood Gate, it was a mere coincidence that you and your ... *friend* came through it?'

'I don't know if it was a coincidence,' said Julie, 'but we didn't do it on purpose. There's a street, you see, in Dublin called Wormwood Gate, probably because that was where one of the old city gates used to be –'

'Enough! I don't want to hear any more of your lies. You are in league with Molly Red and, through her, with the Lord of Shadows. I know this to be true, so it's useless denying it.'

'Then you're not going to believe me, no matter what I say?'

The queen smiled cruelly. 'Tell me the truth and I will believe it. Tell me more lies and I will find a way to make you tell the truth.'

Julie's heart sank. 'What do you want from me?' she said, trying to be brave.

The queen smiled again, this time looking less like a cat with a mouse caught in its claws and more like a shark. 'Why, whatever do you think I want, young lady? I want us to have a nice little chat. I want you to tell me everything you know about the Lord of Shadows and Molly Red and the Queen of Crows. And when we've finished our chat, I want you to go back to your master and tell him that the next time he sends a mortal to threaten me, I'll send that mortal back to him in carved-up pieces. Do you understand?'

'I … think so … but …' Julie hesitated. A horrible thought had occurred to her. 'What are you going to do with Aisling?'

'Who?'

'My …' – *not 'friend', we're not friends, not really* – '… companion.'

'Oh, the other little assassin? Though not so little in her case. Well, she'll be left in her cell until I have a need for her. I may not have a need for her, if you do as I say. Do you understand that?'

Julie nodded, shivering and hugging herself. Yes, she understood: unless she could give the queen satisfactory answers to her questions, bluff convincingly enough at being a spy of the Lord of Shadows (whoever that was), Aisling was in danger. Aisling was a hostage, and if Julie didn't manage to persuade the queen to let both of them go 'back to their master', the queen would do … well, she wasn't sure what the queen would do, but she was pretty sure it would be horrible.

'What do you want to know?' she said.

'Weren't you listening, you tiresome little girl? Everything! I want to know everything!'

'But where should I start? There's so much to tell. I couldn't possibly tell you everything unless you ask me about something more specific.'

The queen strode towards her and slapped her in the face, hard enough to make her eyes water.

'Mind your place, spy,' she hissed. 'Don't be impertinent or you'll get more than a slap next time.'

Julie dropped to her knees, having decided that the queen probably wanted her to grovel. She could do grovelling. Grovelling was easy.

'I beg your forgiveness, Your Majesty,' she said, letting a slight whine enter her voice. 'Whatever you ask, I will answer.'

'That's better,' said the queen. 'But since you were stupid enough to think you could bluff your way past me, perhaps you are also stupid enough to need me to ask for every little thing I want to know. Really, I cannot imagine what possessed the Lord of Shadows to use so incompetent a servant.'

'I don't question the Lord of Shadows,' said Julie, which was true; she could hardly question somebody she'd never met.

'Silence! Don't speak unless you're spoken to. Now, let me see … ' The queen tapped her lips with her forefinger a few times, then turned back around to face out of the windows again. 'First tell me: how did he mean for you to kill me? When, and with what weapons?'

Julie thought for a second, then replied, 'At midnight on the night of the full moon, with a knife made from cold iron.'

She held her breath. Was that the kind of answer the queen was looking for? Was cold iron something you could make a knife out of? Did the City of the Three Castles even *have* a moon?

The queen neither turned nor spoke, merely holding out one hand at her side and gesturing for Julie to continue. Julie exhaled and racked her brain for other colourful notions to present as facts.

'Um … the plan was for me to be the assassin. My companion didn't know what we were supposed to be doing. She was just there to help me … find my way around and … to protect me.'

'Strange for the Lord of Shadows to send two spies and only tell one of them about the nature of their mission.'

'Oh, no, not really, you see –' *think, think, what does she want to hear?* '– the Lord of Shadows knows you to be wise and a … a masterful interrogator. He knew that the less we knew about our mission, the better, so … so only I was told. Aisling didn't need to know for the job to work.'

'That is like him,' murmured the queen, as if she were speaking to herself. Julie glanced back at the horse-head guard, who was watching intently from the back of the room. When their eyes met, he shook his head slightly and looked away.

The queen turned around. 'A knife of cold iron. Traditional, but the Lord of Shadows is a traditional man. His family motto is "What I have, I hold," but it might as well be "If it ain't broke, don't fix it."'

She barked out a dry laugh at this, and Julie summoned a half-hearted, nervous-sounding giggle. The queen raised an eyebrow and smiled, and once more Julie had the uncomfortable feeling of being on the verge of becoming somebody's lunch.

'And the weapon,' said the queen, striding over to the leather chair and seating herself in it without ever moving her eye away from Julie, 'where is it being held? I know you didn't bring it with you, either of you, so don't bother lying and saying you lost it. If cold iron had been brought through the Wormwood Gate, I would know.'

'The … the plan was … to have it forged when we arrived here.'

The queen leaned forward. 'Forged? Are you asking me to believe that you, little puny thing, can swing a blacksmith's hammer? Your companion is made of sturdier stuff, but even she is no smith.'

'No, I meant … someone else is meant to forge it. Someone from here.'

The queen's face went blank. 'Someone … from here?'

'Yes.'

'A citizen of the City of the Three Castles?'

'Yes.'

The queen's eye narrowed. 'Who?'

'Um …' Julie dropped her head, thinking frantically. She had learned a few names along the way – or, rather, not names, since people in this strange place didn't use their real names, but things-to-be-called. She could tell the queen it was The Lungs, except merhorses didn't have hands so they could hardly forge knives. She could tell her it was Jo Maxi, or Prawo Jazdy, or that other one whose name she couldn't pronounce. Or all three of them. *It would serve them right too,* she thought. *They were going to sell us out to the queen; why not let them have a taste of their own medicine?*

She looked up at the queen, who was staring at her with a merciless eye. 'I don't know,' she said.

The queen stood up and walked towards her, her eye boring into Julie's. 'Are you sure?' she said in a sweet, wheedling voice. 'There's no way you could tell me?'

'Like I said,' said Julie, and she could hear the tremble in her own voice now, 'I don't know. The Lord of Shadows didn't –'

The queen grabbed her hair by the crown and dragged her across the carpet to the window, ignoring her struggles and her shrieks of pain. She pushed her up against the window so that her left cheek was squashed against the glass.

'Do you see?' she hissed in Julie's ear. 'Do you see?'

'I – I – wh-what?'

'Do you see a city?'

'I – yes?'

'No, you're wrong. You see *my* city. Mine, do you hear me? Now look down. Straight down.'

She loosened her grip so that Julie could move her head a little. Julie did as she was instructed and looked down, only to see – a cage, was it? Yes, a cage, hanging from what looked like a flagpole sticking out from the side of the tower. It was big enough to hold a person but contained only a bundle of rags.

The queen tapped the glass with her fingernails. It should have just made a clicking noise, but something must have been strange about the glass, because it chimed, as loud and clear as a church bell. The bundle of rags shifted and moved and, to Julie's horror, a single eye looked up from a bruised and emaciated face.

'That is what happened to the last person to oppose me. Do you understand?' the queen said quietly.

'I – I –'

'She was one of three, as was I, until I decided she was too willing to appease the Queen of Crows – too weak and foolish to be allowed to rule. There would be no more of this is-was-will-be nonsense any more. I'd be the one. Me, alone! I am the natural ruler of the city. And so I am, and so I will be. I challenged her in single combat, and when I won the battle, she begged me for the release of death, and I refused. I wanted everyone to know what would happen if they defied me!'

She let go of Julie's head and walked away. Julie peeled her face away from the glass but kept staring down at the shrunken body that had once been a queen. The eye stared up blankly towards her, not seeming to see her or anything else.

I'll help you, Julie thought. Her hands were pressed against the glass in any case, so the queen couldn't see that she was raising one of them to swear an oath. *I'll help you somehow. I'll … I'll find a way to kill you so you can come back different. I swear it!*

She hadn't said the words out loud, but she could feel them affecting her, a tightness gripping first her head, then the rest of her body, just as when she had sworn to leave the City with a better ruler than it had had when she arrived. The blank eye suddenly focused in sharply on hers, and the emaciated face bobbed up and down in a nod.

Oh, crap, Julie thought. *I've got to stop doing that. This is going to make life difficult.*

She turned around, panting slightly, and leaned back against the glass. The queen was seated in the leather chair again, staring impassively at her. 'Have you reconsidered? Do you remember who was to forge this knife for you?'

'I – I was supposed to meet with Molly Red – she knew who it was. I wasn't told. Like I said, the Lord of Shadows only tells his servants what he wants them to know.'

'Molly Red, eh? And when were you to meet that traitor?'

'I … soon after we arrived. But, but, the time for the meeting's long gone now! I don't know where she is. She's … she's probably double-crossed us.'

The queen smiled, a satisfied sort of smile; Julie was half-expecting her to start licking her lips. 'Once a traitor, always a traitor. He shouldn't have trusted her. Not after she betrayed me. Of course, she was his servant before she was mine …' Her eye went distant, and she bit her lip. It was an odd gesture, one that didn't fit the queen's normal posturing at all. 'I had thought that perhaps … Ah, but no. No, that is irrelevant.' Her eye snapped into focus again. 'And was Molly Red to aid you in coming close enough to harm me?'

'Em. No. No, that part we were – I was supposed to figure that out for myself. Perhaps … I thought I'd try corrupting some of your guards.'

The queen laughed. 'And a fine time you would have of it, since my guards are incorruptible! Isn't that right, guard?'

The horse-head guard bowed low and said, 'Of course, Your Majesty. Incorruptible and … *fearless.*'

There was a strange emphasis in the way he said 'fearless', and Julie felt her pulse leaping in her throat. She didn't dare look at the guard, with the queen still facing her, but when the queen swivelled her chair around and strolled over to a drinks cabinet in a corner of the room, Julie risked sending him a questioning glance.

The guard nodded – very slightly, but enough that she was sure she hadn't misunderstood.

'What an incompetent attempt!' the queen said, laughing a little as she poured herself a brightly coloured drink. 'What must the Lord of Shadows be … thinking …' Her voice trailed off and she pivoted smoothly on her heels, still holding the glass and the bottle, one in each hand. She stared at Julie with a blank expression for a moment that stretched out like chewing gum. Julie did her best to look gormless and uninformed. The queen tilted her head to one side, narrowed her eye, then shook her head with a chuckle and returned to her drink. 'No, not you. If he has another plan – and if I know the Lord of Shadows at all, he has more than one – you are not part of it. Not wise enough. Not clever enough. Not strong enough.'

Julie wanted to protest, but there was too much at stake. 'Now that I've told you what I know,' she said in as humble a tone as she could manage, 'what will you do?'

The queen carried her drink to the chair and arranged herself in it so that one of her legs was hanging over one arm; to a casual glance the pose would look artless and lazy, but Julie could see that the queen could leap up from it in an eye-blink and go on the attack.

'What shall I do?' the queen murmured, as if to herself. 'What shall I do with a wayward spy, a failed assassin, an incompetent servant of my enemy? Why, whatever shall I do? So many uses I could put you to.' She giggled – a light, sweet sound that made Julie shiver, coming out of that cruel mouth. 'So many ways I could punish you.'

When Julie was in primary school, her class had done a project on earthworms. Most of the class had been very dutiful in keeping and caring for their designated earthworms, but there had been a few boys and one or two girls who had taken pleasure in pricking them with pins, cutting them in two, tossing them about, leaving them exposed to air so that they dried out and died. It was the squirming they liked most. The more the worms moved, the more they looked like they were in pain, the more these children liked it.

I won't be your worm, Julie thought as the queen's eye watched her and the edges of her mouth slipped downwards. *I gave you what you wanted, but I won't be your worm!*

The queen abruptly shifted her body in the chair so that she was sitting upright and tossed back her drink in one swallow. 'Very well,' she said, slamming the glass down on the table next to the chair. 'How loyal are you to the Lord of Shadows?'

'I'm not really loyal to him at all,' said Julie, quite pleased to be able to tell the truth.

'And your companion?'

'It's the same for her. We're … you could say we sort of fell into this. We don't really care what happens to the Lord of Shadows or his plans.'

'Excellent,' said the queen, steepling her fingers, and the word and the gesture together reminded Julie so much of Mr Burns from *The Simpsons* that she had to bite the insides of her cheeks to keep from laughing. 'In that case,' the queen went on, 'you won't object to working against him. Will you?' Julie shook her head. 'Marvellous. Then I give you the following task: find Molly Red. Find out her plan. Find out whether she is still working for the Lord of Shadows; if she's not, find out who she is working for. Find these things out, and tell what you have learned to me or one of my loyal servants – and if you're not sure if the servant is loyal, assume he is not. Do you understand?'

Julie nodded. 'And … what if I can't? Molly Red's pretty cunning. I might not be able to find her.'

'You will find her. Or she'll find you. She has a way of knowing when she's being sought, which is why some people have great trouble finding her, but she's curious enough that she'll want to know why you're looking for her. Seek her with audacity, with persistence, with care, with diligence, and she will make herself known to you.'

'I understand,' said Julie, 'but what if I fail?'

The queen smiled. Julie was beginning to hate the

sight of the queen's smile. 'Your "companion" … I think you'd be sorry if anything *unpleasant* were to happen to her. Am I correct?'

Julie gasped and immediately cursed her foolishness; the queen's smile had broadened, and her eye was glittering with mirth. 'Of course I am,' the queen went on. 'I pride myself on my judgement of character. Yes, you and your … companion … you did claim that she knew nothing of your original mission; it would be foolish, then, to involve her in this new one. Don't you agree?' The smile vanished. 'She stays in the cells until you return with accurate intelligence about Molly Red. After one moonrise with no information, I'll stop feeding her. After three, I'll release rats into her cell. Very *hungry* rats. Do you understand?'

'Yes!' Julie cried, no longer bothering to pretend she didn't care.

'Very well,' said the queen. She snapped her fingers. 'Guard! Escort this spy to the exit, and inform the Seagull Patrol and the Dog Patrols to watch out for her. She is working for me, but she is not to be trusted.'

The horse-head guard bowed, although the queen couldn't see him from where she was sitting, and marched over to where Julie was standing. He made a face which Julie thought might have been apologetic – on a horse's face, it was hard to tell – and lifted her up over his shoulder in a fireman's carry.

Julie was too worn out to protest. She lay passively on his shoulder as he carried her through the queen's chamber, along the short corridor, and down the spiral staircase, until they were at a point that she thought was about halfway between the queen's floor and the ground, when he set her down carefully on a step.

'Are you going to help me?' she said before he could speak.

'I'd rather not,' he said with a sigh, 'because no matter how many sandwiches short of a picnic your woman upstairs might be, she's still the queen, and she'll go through me for a shortcut if she finds out.'

'But you want to, don't you? You want to be fearless.'

The guard looked away. 'We're none of us happy with head-the-ball in charge of the city,' he muttered. 'She's knocking down houses and building new ones twice as big and ten times as ugly, and us guards are run ragged just trying to keep up with the patrols.' He looked at her. 'You were telling the truth the first time, weren't you? Yous two did come to the City by accident.'

'Yes,' said Julie. 'But that doesn't mean I don't want to help. I want to go home, but … I want to make things better first.'

'Will you swear to it?'

'I already have,' said Julie. 'I swore I wouldn't leave the City until it had a better ruler than it had when I arrived, and I swore I'd help the old queen – the Queen-that-was, is that what you call her? The one in the cage – that I'd find a way to kill her so she could come back –'

Before she could finish, the guard grabbed her upper arms and laughed delightedly, a delightful sound after the queen's dry, mirthless, mocking, cruel laugh. 'You swore to that? Sure, we're away in a hack! An oath like that will find a way to come true.'

'You're sure?'

'Sure as sure can be. Come on.' He turned around and crouched down. 'I'll give you a piggyback the rest of the way. We're going to visit your friend in the cells.'

Julie climbed up on his back. 'And set her free?'

'Of course,' said the guard, jogging down the stairs. 'Sure, when your friend is free, you'll have a loose leg, won't you?'

'Em, I suppose so.' Julie didn't know what 'a loose leg' meant, but this was not the time to ask for definitions. 'And you won't tell the patrols?'

'Ah. Well, now. Now that you mention that … I'm going to have to, though I'd rather not.'

'If you'd rather not, why do you have to?'

'Your woman'll find out, and soon enough to make trouble for you and your friend,' said the guard, 'and more trouble for me. No, I'll have to tell them, but I'll do you this favour: I'll dawdle and delay until the last moment. You should have a head start of ten minutes at least, and that's enough time to get to places where they won't find you.'

'If you say so,' Julie muttered.

They reached the bottom of the stairs, and the guard crouched down. 'You can walk the rest of the way, since you're supposed to be working for the queen.'

Julie shook out her legs quickly and started down towards the corridor where her and Aisling's cell was, with the guard following behind her. At the corner, they ran into a patrol and had to squash themselves against the wall to let the other guards march past, with Julie all the while bowing her head and hoping that none of them would guess that anything was amiss. When the last booted foot had long passed and their footsteps couldn't be heard any more, she let out a breath and ran down the corridor towards the cell, then skidded to a halt when she realised that she didn't know which cell had been hers.

The guard pushed past her gently and strode towards one cell in particular.

'This one,' he said.

He took out a ring of keys and unlocked the door, then pulled back the bolt and flung the door open.

'You've got it wrong,' said Julie. 'This isn't our cell. It's empty.'

The guard sniffed the air. 'It's empty now,' he said, 'but it smells of you and your friend. This was your cell all right.'

'Then where … Are you asking me to believe that Aisling's disappeared into thin air?'

'Or escaped,' said the guard. 'With the help of somebody less fearful than me.'

'I don't believe it,' Julie said, stepping into the cell and looking around, her eyes sweeping the walls and the floor. 'I haven't even been gone that long, how could she –'

She broke off what she was about to say. Her eyes had fallen on a small oblong object that looked thoroughly out of place in the cell with its stone walls and straw-strewn floor. It was so dark that it almost faded out of view, but when Julie picked it up, it lit up.

'You're right,' said Julie flatly, staring at the screen of Aisling's mobile phone. 'This was our cell. And Aisling's escaped.'

The guard was silent for a moment, then put a hand on her shoulder. 'Then there's no need to worry about her. Come on, I have to take you to the exit.'

5

Aisling slumped down onto the bench after the door slammed shut. She didn't like the fact that the guard had called her fat (okay, so her body mass index was outside the recommended range, but she was still growing and it had never caused any health problems), but that was just a minor irritant next to the way he'd dragged Julie away. To see the queen, he'd said, as if that was meant to be reassuring. As if it hadn't been the queen who'd locked them away in the first place.

If it hadn't been so damp and cold in the cell, and if she weren't on the verge of a panic attack, it might have been funny; after all, she'd always wanted to travel to a magical land, and she'd always secretly liked the idea of being locked up as a political prisoner, and now she was doing both at the same time, and it was turning out to be … well, *interesting*, sure, but not exactly fun.

As if someone had heard that she liked swords and also liked cats, and had given her a cat impaled on a sword.

She picked up her phone, climbed up onto the bench and peered through the window. There were streaks of pink and orange in the patch of sky that was visible; the light was still dim and diffuse, but the sun would be all the way up soon. She couldn't help wondering whether the City would still be there when the sun rose. Would she wake up to find it had all been a dream? Or would the City of the Three Castles dissolve in the sunlight, leaving only the Dublin she had always known?

Her train of thought was interrupted by a pair of bright red eyes staring directly into hers from the other side of the window.

'Howaya?' said the owner of the eyes, who appeared to be a rabbit.

'Um,' said Aisling. 'I, um … I suppose I'm all right, considering. And yourself?'

'Not too bad, not too bad. Would you be a prisoner, by any chance?'

'Well … yes.'

'And would you be happy being a prisoner? Mind you, I'm only asking.'

'Of course I'm not happy,' said Aisling. 'What kind of stupid question is that?'

'Well, then,' said the rabbit in a considering sort of

way, 'would you be willing to help a body out, if a body could help you out, no pun intended?'

'You … are you saying you can get me out of here?'

'That I am, and that I can. Interested?'

'What do you want in exchange?' said Aisling cautiously. It was dangerous to make promises in this place.

'You and your friend came through the Wormwood Gate, didn't yous?'

'How did you know that?'

'Word travels fast in this place. Almost as fast as the Gate. I've been looking for it, you see, and I reckon if I could find a place where it was open, I could track it down by nose. All you'd have to do is take me to the place where you and your friend came through.'

'And if I do this, you can get me out of this prison?'

The rabbit winked. It was a very peculiar sight. 'These paws and whiskers know a trick or two. I can have you out of there before you blink. Well, what's it to be?'

Aisling bit her lip as she pondered her new options. On the one hand, she didn't want to leave Julie behind; on the other hand, hanging around in a cell doing nothing in particular wasn't helping Julie at all. On the third hand, did she really trust this rabbit? On the fourth hand, it wasn't as if she trusted the queen either. On the fifth hand, she really, really, *really* didn't want to leave Julie behind. On the sixth hand, if it worked out – which was, admittedly, a big 'if' – maybe she'd be able to rescue Julie. She liked that idea. Swooping down in the nick of time to sweep her up out of the arms of the villain …

Well, it wouldn't be like that, of course. Not *exactly* like that, anyway. But …

Aisling looked at the rabbit. She had no idea what an untrustworthy rabbit would look like, if there even was such a thing as an untrustworthy rabbit. She had a cousin who had a pet rabbit which was vicious when provoked and had a tendency to chew cables if left unsupervised, but that didn't make it untrustworthy in any meaningful sense. 'Do you *swear* you'll get me out of prison?'

The rabbit chuckled. 'Oh, no, you won't catch me that way! I'm saying nothing till you say you'll help. Well, will you help?'

'I'll help if you get me out of here! And if you promise not to pull any funny business once I'm free.'

The rabbit stretched its head forward. 'What do you mean by "funny business"?'

'Like, for example, selling me back to the queen's guards.'

'I can swear not to do that easy enough, since I wasn't going to do it anyway,' said the rabbit. 'Are we agreed, then? I let you out of prison, you help me find the Gate, and once I find it we part ways all friends together?'

'That sounds acceptable,' Aisling said, nodding. 'How are you going to get me out of here?'

'Step down and away from the window,' said the rabbit. 'It'll be done in a jiff.'

Aisling jumped down from the bench and backed away a few feet, her eyes fixed on the rabbit, which was just barely visible now that her face was more than a couple of inches away from it. There was a deep thumping noise, and then a high-pitched whirr, and the bars of the window somehow melted into the stones above and underneath them, and the stones themselves shrunk down or squeezed up so that the window was twice its former size – still a tight squeeze, but big enough to let her through, leather coat and all.

'Wow,' she said, for want of anything more intelligent to say. She climbed back up onto the bench and was on the verge of pulling herself up through the window when she remembered Julie and thought of leaving her a note. She immediately dismissed that as a stupid idea, because if Julie could read the note, so could the guards. She glanced at the phone in her hand, quickly typed a text message and saved it in the outbox, then carefully placed the phone on the bench, screen-side-up. She hadn't seen anything like a mobile phone from the moment they'd arrived, and she was pretty sure the guards weren't technologically savvy enough to figure out how to use one without help.

'Right,' she said, more to herself than to the rabbit,

though the rabbit nodded and hopped backwards to make room for her. She grabbed onto the ledge and pulled herself up, squirming and twisting her body to fit through the window. It was a bit of a scramble, but she made it fairly easily, and once she was out, she could see that there was a clear path between the window and the nearest gate.

'They're changing the guard,' said the rabbit, loping off towards the gate. 'We'd best hurry.'

Aisling followed it, a little unnerved to realise that even though it was an ordinary-looking rabbit of an ordinary size, it was moving fast enough that she had trouble keeping up. They ran through the gate and through the streets, and they didn't stop running for what felt like half an hour, though when they finally stopped the sun hadn't moved enough for it to have been more than a few minutes. Aisling leaned against the nearest wall to catch her breath, while the rabbit flopped to the ground and panted noisily.

'Well,' Aisling said once her lungs had recovered, 'what's the next step?'

The rabbit pulled itself to its feet, a little unsteadily.

'Introductions,' it said. 'You can call me Coney Bawn. What can I call you?'

'My name's – actually, you could just call me "friend",' said Aisling.

'Fair enough,' said the rabbit approvingly. 'Now, do you remember how you came into the City?'

'We didn't do anything,' said Aisling. 'We were on a street called Wormwood Gate, and Ju – my friend and I were just standing there, and suddenly there was a really strong smell of – well, we weren't sure, but I thought it was wormwood. I have an interest in herbalism, you see, so a while ago when I was in London I went to … well, anyway, that's not really relevant. The point is, a moment later a white horse with a red mane appeared out of nowhere and knocked us down –'

'A white horse with a red mane?'

'Yes. And then when we got up, we were here. Or,' she glanced around at the dead-end alleyway they'd ended up in, 'not here, exactly, but here in the City. Near the riverbank.'

'Which side of the River?'

'Ehmm …' Aisling tried to remember. It had been such a shock, and they'd hardly had a moment to catch a breath, much less orient themselves properly and figure out which way was north. Normally when she was lost in the city centre, she just kept walking until she could see the Spire, and then she would know.

She gasped. 'The Tower of Light!'

'Yes,' said the rabbit with some irritation, 'that's where we've just come from, but where were you before then?'

'The Tower was across the river from where we were. We're on the Northside now, aren't we? When the seagulls took us to the Tower, they must have flown us across the river.'

'Had to,' said the rabbit grimly. 'The queen's shut off most of the bridges, even for official business. Well, that narrows it down, but I haven't a notion how we're going to get to where you were. I can do a lot of things with these paws and whiskers, but flying isn't one of them.'

'Could we cross by boat?'

'Be boat? Are you mad?' said the rabbit. 'There's only one boat goes across the River, and it's only the dead can ride in it. That's you ruled out, for starters. I could go, if I was willing to die and take me chances in the next life, but I'm not so sure I am, with things the way they are. There's rumours the queen is even trying to control that.'

'Control what? Death?'

'No, no – not even the Queen of Crows controls death. *She* calls herself the queen of death, but even she's not that powerful. No, no, I mean what happens *after* you die.'

'Wait, back up a minute. There's a boat that only the dead can ride in? What's that about?'

'We folk of the Realms Between aren't like yous mortals,' said the rabbit. 'We can die, but when we die we go to the banks of the River and the Ferryman takes us across, back to the Realm where we died. Only, crossing the River changes us. The Ferryman decides how. At least, for the Fae folk. For the in-betweeners, they have enough of their own selves that all he can do is give them a new shape to choose from. He can't take away their old shape.'

Aisling digested this. 'And the queen wants to control the Ferryman?'

The rabbit made a motion with its paws that was sort of like a shrug.

'There's rumours. I don't think much of them, meself. The Ferryman's bound to serve the Queen of Crows. He has some liberty in what he does, but not much. Not enough to go free by himself, and not enough to choose a different mistress.'

'And this river – the river you cross after dying – that's the same as the river in the City?'

The rabbit cocked its head to one side. 'It is and it isn't,' it said. 'The Ferryman's river has no bridges over it, and it flows through every city and every town and every village, not just the City of the Three Castles. But the River in the City is the Ferryman's river all the same.'

'I don't get it,' said Aisling. 'I mean, are you saying they're the same river but they exist in different dimensions or something?'

'I don't know what you mean,' said the rabbit. 'The Ferryman's river is not the River in the City, but the River in the City is the Ferryman's river. Except when it isn't. You follow me?'

'Not in the slightest,' Aisling sighed, 'but I suppose it doesn't matter. So the Ferryman doesn't work for the Queen of the City, then?'

'No, and a good thing too.'

'Is "the Ferryman" his true name?' said Aisling. 'It seems like a strange sort of name for a person to have.'

'I don't rightly know that he *is* a person,' said the rabbit, tilting its head to one side. 'But either way, it's not just true names that have power. A make-name can be powerful too. I know a creature called Abayomiolorunkoje –'

'I've met him!' Aisling exclaimed.

'I bet you have,' said the rabbit. 'He's got more faces than a mask shop, that one. He gets around more than you'd guess. Anyhow, that's not his name for real and true, but he tells everyone in the City to call him that, and he tells them what it means.'

'"People wanted to humiliate me, but God would not let them."'

'Exactly! And what do you think happens any time people try to make him feel like he's got too big for his breeches?'

'I think I can imagine.'

The rabbit nodded. 'It's always a different thing, but *something* always happens. Something that looks like a coincidence. Some people even think it is, but I know better. It's that he's said it often enough that it's becoming true: people tried to humiliate him, but God wouldn't let them.'

'Maybe not God,' Aisling muttered, for she had been an atheist since she was nine. 'Anyway. If "the Ferryman" is his make-name – is it as powerful as his real name?'

The rabbit shook its head, then frowned. 'I don't rightly know,' it said. 'The thing of it is, a make-name you choose can't be used against you. You have control over it, see? It's your way of telling the world what you want to be. That's why nobody can shorten it for you: they don't have the power over it that you do. But a true name is something else altogether. A true name is the world's way of telling you what you are, whether you like it or not. If I knew the Ferryman's true name, I'd know what he was for true, and then I'd have power over him. But every time a person says his make-name, they're telling the world that he is what he wants to be. If that happened often enough, for long enough, maybe it'd be his true name for real.'

'I see,' said Aisling thoughtfully, and for once she actually thought she did see. The world she and Julie had fetched up in was fluid, almost as if it were unsure of itself. A strong mind could poke it into a different shape just by willing it. But not any old shape; there had to be rules, limits to what a mind could do, or else the City would have no form at all. 'Where do mortals fit into all this?' she said, adding, 'If we're going to find the Gate, I need to know what I can do and what I can't.'

'I don't rightly know,' said the rabbit with an air of dejection. 'I was sort of hoping you'd know, being one yourself. But of course you're a blow-in – you've no more notion of why the queen was hunting you than me left hind paw.'

'I just wonder,' she said, 'if the – I don't know if it's accurate to call them "rules", exactly – the underlying mechanism around names … does that even apply to me? Do I even *have* a true name? I mean, this place, it's like Dublin, kind of, but the real Tower of Light is just a big spike in the middle of a street. It makes a good landmark if you're lost, but there isn't room inside it to fit a single cell, much less a whole prison.'

The rabbit looked confused. 'What do you mean, real? This *is* real.'

Aisling sighed. 'I suppose it is, at that. Real enough, at least. But …' She was on the verge of saying, 'Where I come from, you can't change a person's life just by changing their name,' but she wasn't sure enough of that to say it out loud. You could even change the spelling of a name, and that would make a difference. Her second favourite singer was called Siouxsie Sioux, not Suzy Sue.

She crept to the edge of the alley, keeping close to the wall, and peered out. 'We're near the river,' she whispered. 'Do you suppose we could swim? People do swim in the river, sometimes.' *Very masochistic people*, she added in her head.

117

'Not *people*,' said the rabbit quietly. 'Merhorses and the dead. Though I suppose you couldn't call what the dead do "swimming".'

There has to be a way, said Aisling to herself. To the rabbit, she said, 'What's the deal about the Wormwood Gate, anyway?'

The rabbit made another of those movements that might have been a shrug. 'It moves. It's the only gate that moves, so the queen can't close it or keep a guard on it. It was still for a while, but then it started moving again. It disappeared for a bit, and there was rumours that the queen had destroyed it, though I didn't credit them. She's powerful, but not *that* powerful.'

'Is there another way to cross the river?' said Aisling. 'Any bridges the queen doesn't know about, or –'

'There's one bridge she can't set a guard on,' said the rabbit, 'but you can't cross it on foot. It's a railway bridge, and there's trains going back and forth on it all the time.'

'Could we catch one of those trains?'

'Do I look like I carry train fare in me pockets?'

'Well, how much would it be? Or … do we absolutely need a fare? I mean, I've fare-dodged a couple of times when I didn't have money on me, and it's not that hard.'

The rabbit gave her a hard stare.

'You must have a brass neck,' it said after a long pause, 'to want to blag a free ride on the trains with the queen on the rampage and you not half an hour out of prison!' It laughed a slightly wheezy laugh that went on for a long time, and when the laugh finally died down, it nodded and hopped towards her until it was crouched at her feet. 'Let's chance our arms,' it said. 'The worst that can happen me is I get reborn as a slug or something. I don't know what the worst would be for you, but you don't seem to care, so what matter? Pick me up, would you? Me legs is tired.'

Aisling bent to pick the rabbit up. 'Where's the nearest station?' she said as she straightened up.

The rabbit peered around, sniffing the air. 'This way,' it said, indicating the right direction with its head. 'I'll give you a steer if it gets complicated.'

Aisling started to walk in the direction the rabbit had indicated, hoping that it wouldn't be too far a walk; the rabbit was heavier than it looked, and her own legs were pretty tired. She was tired in general, for that matter; she had got no sleep at all, and between the climbing and the running and the stress and the excitement, she felt she'd done more in the … however long it had been … that she'd spent in the City than she'd normally do in a year.

She looked around as she walked, trying to get a better sense of what the City was like. Now that the sun was rising and she had an idea of what to look for, she could see that the City was not as much like Dublin as it had seemed by night – or rather, it was much *more* like

119

Dublin than it had seemed by night, more like Dublin than Dublin itself, as if the boring and generic bits of Dublin had been filtered out and only the unique and interesting bits had been left behind. There were no chain stores here, no blandly inoffensive bars, no fast-food restaurants, no billboards; there were precious few new buildings, despite what the rabbit had said. Everything she saw seemed refined, simplified, like a drawing of itself, or a photograph that had had all the distracting extraneous details airbrushed out.

She peeked down at the rabbit, warm and silent in her arms. It looked a little unreal too, now that she was looking at it properly. *And why a rabbit?* she thought. *How does that make sense?*

They came to an area she recognised as being near the Four Courts, and then with a jolt she realised that the vaguely silhouetted building she'd been seeing peeking over the tops of the houses *was* the Four Courts. It wasn't that any of the details of the building's structure or design were different – it had the same dome, the same pillars, the same imposing grandeur – but somehow in the dawning light of the City of the Three Castles, it looked … sinister. Frightening. When she'd passed it by in Dublin, she'd always been able to admire it as a work of architecture, but now she could only think of the number of times people must have gone in there hoping to be cleared of crimes they hadn't committed and had their hopes dashed; and the people too who must have gone in there hoping that a person who had done them some terrible wrong would be punished for it and been bitterly disappointed.

'Here,' said the rabbit. It was quivering in Aisling's arms, its eyes darting around. Aisling glanced around, spotted two sets of tracks running in parallel down the middle of the street, a small platform with a sign saying FOUR COURTS – *Na Ceithre Cúirteanna* and a very uncomfortable-looking bench. She sat down on the bench to wait and started stroking the rabbit absent-mindedly. It occurred to her a moment after she'd started that this might be an unforgivable liberty, but the rabbit didn't seem to mind, so she didn't stop.

'This is a Luas station,' she said after a while, 'not a train station. That's no good to us if we want to cross a railway bridge.'

'You wha'?' said the rabbit. 'Lewis? What are you on about?'

'Huh,' said Aisling, 'never mind; it doesn't matter.'

There was a familiar *clang clang clang*, and Aisling stood up as a tram approached. Or was it a train? She couldn't tell. It had the shape of a Luas tram, but the colouring of a DART train. The effect was very disconcerting. The doors too were a weird hybrid of DART and Luas doors, and there was a gap between the train (tram?) and the platform that was deeper and wider than it should have been.

She took a window seat in a set of four and put the rabbit down on the seat beside her. There were a few other passengers, all of them odd – though by now that was what she had come to expect. One was a ragged old man wearing what looked like multiple overcoats layered one on top of the other, muttering to himself. One was a middle-aged woman dressed all in black, her hand resting on the handlebar of a pram full of vegetables, singing the Schubert 'Ave Maria' in a cracked and melancholy voice. One was a tall, thin man with a face made up like a clown, wearing an ankle-length white fur coat and riding a unicycle back and forth from one end of the tram to the other.

She was a little disappointed that there were no talking animals or other mythological creatures to be seen, but perhaps it was too early in the day.

The woman with the pram got out at the first stop, and the rabbit bumped Aisling's arm with its nose.

'Lift me up to the map there,' it said. 'I want to be sure we don't get off too early.'

Aisling obeyed, taking a good look at the map herself. It confirmed her suspicion: whatever the reason, the City of the Three Castles didn't distinguish between the DART, the Luas, and any other train that happened to pass through Dublin; they were all smooshed together to form one uber-rail service, which made the map a little complicated to read.

'Tara Street,' said the rabbit quietly. 'Is that near where yous got dropped off?'

'I don't think so,' said Aisling, just as quietly. 'It's on the right side of the river, but we were further west down the quays.'

'Ah, bejaysus, more walkin',' said the rabbit. 'Ach, I suppose it can't be helped. But I've a powerful hatred for walkin' more than fifty feet. It's not dignified, sure it's not.'

'You're a rabbit after my own heart,' said Aisling, who never walked anywhere if she could get away with it.

'Tickets please!' cried a voice, and Aisling's heart began to pound. She sat down and tucked the rabbit under her coat, folding her arms over the bulge this formed and closing her eyes. *I'm not here*, she thought fervently, *and if I am here, you already checked my ticket. I'm not here, and if I am, you already checked my ticket. Oh, if I believed in God I'd be praying right now!*

Another voice cried, 'Tickets please!', this time in a Polish accent, coming from another direction. Aisling opened her eyes and darted a look back over her shoulder. Prawo Jazdy was approaching them from behind, wearing a startlingly yellow high-visibility jacket over a dark blue uniform, ticket clipper in one hand, smartcard verifier in the other. She glanced in the other direction, and saw Abayomiolorunkoje, in an identical uniform, coming towards them from the other end of the train.

'Well, isn't this a fine to-do,' the rabbit muttered, poking its head out from between the flaps of Aisling's coat. 'Though there's few enough people in the City these days that a thing like this was bound to happen.'

'What do you –'

'Shh! I'll do the talking.'

Abayomiolorunkoje reached them first. He gave them both an assessing look. Aisling wasn't sure whether she felt more scared of what he might do or more creeped out by the odd way his eyes reflected the light. 'I suppose you do not have a ticket, do you, Coney Bawn?'

'Sure why would I want one, when I know me old butty Abayomiolorunkoje is always happy to give me a scooch?' said the rabbit.

Abayomiolorunkoje looked from Aisling to the rabbit and back again. Aisling held her head straight, though it was an effort not to look away or lower her gaze from those strange eyes. *I didn't do anything wrong*, she thought, *so I'm not going to act guilty.*

'What is going on?' said Prawo Jazdy, coming up alongside their seat. 'Ah!' he cried when he saw Aisling. 'You got away! You have not been caught?'

'I don't see why I should tell you anything about that,' said Aisling. 'You two, and your friend, you were going to sell us to the queen. Are you going to do that now? Whistle for the seagulls and have us carried away to the Tower?'

Abayomiolorunkoje took a step back. 'No need to be hasty,' he said. 'Why don't we –'

'No need!' Prawo Jazdy shouted. 'How can you say no need?' He threw his clipper and his verifier to the floor with a clatter and reached for Aisling as if he was going to lift her out of her seat and toss her over his shoulder. Aisling wrapped her arms around the rabbit, pulling it close to her chest and shrinking down into her seat.

And between one blink and the next, Prawo Jazdy disappeared.

Aisling's mouth fell open. 'What …' Her voice was hoarse. She cleared her throat and tried again. 'What just happened? Coney Bawn, did you do that?'

The rabbit shook its head vigorously. 'That wasn't me,' it said in a quiet, scared-sounding voice.

'Nor me,' said Abayomiolorunkoje, though he didn't look scared so much as grimly resigned, as if this had confirmed the truth of something he'd been fearing for a long time.

'Then what …' Aisling loosened her arms a little. She could feel the rabbit's heart pounding against its ribs, even through all the fur. 'What was that?'

'That was the City fading a little,' said Abayomiolorunkoje.

'I've never seen it with me own eyes,' said the rabbit. 'Usually you look away, and it's when you look back that things have changed. Or gone.'

'It has been happening more and more,' said Abayomiolorunkoje. 'To people, to buildings ... whole streets have been vanishing before my eyes.'

'And what would you care about that?' said the rabbit, its tone sharper than Aisling had ever heard it. 'Sure, you're not a Betweener.'

'He's not?' said Aisling.

'What does that matter?' Abayomiolorunkoje said. 'The Realms Between have no native-born children, only those who pass through and make a home here. I have wandered far from my homeland, and you have too, I think. I can care about a realm that is not my own. I like this City. At least, I used to like it. It was once a fine place to sit and spin a web. I would rather not see it destroyed.'

'That's not what you said last night,' said Aisling. She was only half following the conversation, but what she could pick up didn't seem to accord with what she had overheard Abayomiolorunkoje saying to the others the night before.

Abayomiolorunkoje shrugged. 'The sun has risen, and the world is different,' he said, taking off his cap and scratching his head. 'Soon, either the queen will fall or the City will collapse. It cannot survive long in the Realms Between as it is.'

'This girl's trying to stop that from happening,' said the rabbit, and Aisling nodded.

Abayomiolorunkoje put his cap back on and

exhaled sharply. 'If I can help you in any way that is in my power, I will come if you call for me. That is a promise! And if I cannot help you, call for me all the same. There are creatures scattered through all the Realms Between who owe me favours and will come when they hear my name.'

From the solemnity of his expression, Aisling was sure that the promise was binding – just as binding as the promise she'd made to the floating head. Perhaps that was the reason why Abayomiolorunkoje had given himself such a long make-name – the harder it was for people to call for him, the fewer such promises he would have to fulfil.

'We don't need you now,' said the rabbit, 'but if we do, we know how to get you.'

Abayomiolorunkoje nodded. 'Good luck to you both!' he said and walked on down the carriage.

'That could've been worse,' said the rabbit.

Aisling nodded and looked out the window. The train was crossing the river now, over a bridge that was almost exactly like the DART bridge, but not quite. 'We're nearly there,' she said, and a moment later a cultivated female voice announced, *'The next station is Tara Street. An chéad stáisiún eile, Sráid Teamhrach,'* and the train pulled in to Tara Street Station. Coney wriggled out of her grasp and leapt to the floor, then hopped out of the train to the platform. 'Come on!' it cried, and Aisling scrambled after it.

'Coney Bawn,' she said as they walked along the quays, 'do you mind telling me something?'

'Depends what it is.'

'It's just that you're a white rabbit, and your make-name is "Coney Bawn". Doesn't that just mean "white rabbit"?'

The rabbit stopped its slow loping and looked up at her, a twinkle in its eye. 'What did I tell you? A real name tells you who you are. A make-name tells the world who you want to be.'

'Who you – oh. So you're not – but if you're not a rabbit, what are you?'

The rabbit winked, which looked just as odd now as it had done before. 'That'd be telling.'

Aisling rolled her eyes and resumed walking in the vague direction of Wormwood Gate. 'Why does everyone here have to be so *bloody enigmatic*?' she muttered.

The rabbit ignored that remark, if it even heard at all, and just lolloped along beside her, occasionally pointing out things that had changed since the queen had taken the throne – mostly areas of waste ground where there had once been fine old buildings and were now building sites and brand new buildings all made of concrete and shiny glass. The new buildings seemed to shimmer as she looked at them, as if they hadn't quite made up their minds whether or not to exist. Aisling thought she understood that: if the City was a reflection of Dublin, or of what people thought and felt about Dublin, it stood to reason that new buildings that hadn't had time to be loved or hated or feared wouldn't seem as real here as the ones that had been around for centuries.

Though that didn't explain how the Spire had been turned into a prison. Perhaps the queen had enough willpower to transform it all by herself.

They came at last – by a somewhat roundabout route, and with much ducking into doorways and under arches to avoid guard patrols – to the stretch of the quays where Aisling remembered talking to the merhorse.

'It was near here,' she said. 'I don't know where exactly – it was such a shock, I wasn't in the best state to take notes. But definitely somewhere near here. A little to the south, away from the river.'

'Good!' said the rabbit. 'I was hoping you'd remember.'

Aisling started. The rabbit's voice sounded different; where it had been high and squeaky and androgynous, it was mellow now, a woman's voice. 'What – are you –'

Coney loped off towards an alleyway, and Aisling followed, too astonished to wonder whether that was a good idea. When she reached the mouth of the alley, she was just in time to see Coney transform from a small white rabbit into a red-haired woman in a white hoodie and white tracksuit trousers.

'Sorry about that,' said the woman, 'but I couldn't be sure you'd take me where I needed to go if I told you everything. Now, let's dispense with make-names, shall we? You're Aisling O'Riordan. And I'm Molly Red.'

She held out her right hand. Aisling shook it, trying to disguise the way her own hand was trembling.

'Molly Red, eh?' she said. 'I've heard of you.'

6

The guard was silent as he led Julie to the gate. No matter how many times she whispered a plea for help, his jaw stayed clamped shut and he gave no more response than a small, firm shake of his head. She had no idea where she might find Molly Red, if she was even still in the City, or how she could track where Aisling had gone, or whether there was anyone in the City who could help her, so as soon as he left her at the gate she broke into a run, heading in a random direction, just wanting to put as much distance as possible between herself and the Tower of Light.

A dozen or more streets away, her foot slipped out of her shoe and she skidded to a halt, just barely stopping herself from falling flat on her face. She leaned against the nearest wall for a moment, panting and rotating her ankle, and looked around to see where she was.

She didn't recognise the area at all: the alley she was in was high and narrow enough to block her view of any landmarks, and the buildings were of a kind that she couldn't remember seeing anywhere in Dublin – she had seen houses like that in English towns, Tudor or older, with low eaves and exposed wooden beams everywhere, but as far as she knew there were none in Dublin; they'd all been knocked down to make way for new ones in the eighteenth century.

That had to mean that this was a part of the City that came from the past.

Julie slipped her shoe back on and looked up at the sky. It should have been brighter, but there were dark clouds massing – not rain clouds: smoke clouds, thick and black and acrid-smelling. She must have been near one of the burning castles, then; and if this part of the city came from the past, perhaps it was the castle that had belonged to the Queen-that-was …

What kind of logic is that? she thought to herself, irritated. But she had nothing else to go on, and that seemed to be how the City worked, in any case, as if it wasn't held together by the laws of physics so much as by chewing gum and good intentions. And now that the queen had no good intentions at all, it was beginning to fall apart.

She sniffed the air and set off in the direction the smoke seemed to be coming from. The streets in this part of the City were narrow and twisty, paved with irregular cobblestones when they were paved at all, and it seemed that every time she thought she was going straight in the right direction she would run smack into a dead end and have to retrace her steps. The fourth time this happened, she picked up a stone and scraped an X into the dead-end wall, just to make sure she wasn't going around in circles, only to find that when she looked back over her shoulder at it, the X had disappeared. At that, she flopped down onto the ground and groaned.

'What did I ever do to you, eh?' she muttered, glaring at the houses and the cobblestones and the billowing smoke in the sky. 'I don't know why you have a grudge against me, City, but it's getting really boring.'

The cobblestones did not reply. Julie sighed and stood up again. 'Lateral thinking,' she said to herself. 'What would Aisling do?' She looked up again and noticed something she hadn't seen before: there were telephone wires stretched between the houses. They looked very strange, juxtaposed with all that Tudor-or-was-it-medieval architecture; there was even a pair of runners slung over one of them, hanging by the laces.

Julie stretched up on the tips of her toes, her eyes narrowing. The runners were white, but the laces were red. Not something you would see unless you were looking closely. And was that the tongue of the left shoe sticking out, or a piece of paper with writing on it? The more she looked at it, the more sure she was that it was a piece of paper, and the more she thought about it, the more sure she was that a piece of paper stuffed into a pair of white runners with red laces hanging from a telephone wire could only be some kind of message.

She glanced at the house behind her. It looked gratifyingly climbable; she'd never had the chance to climb a medieval-or-possibly-Tudor house before, but with its low eaves, thatched roof (not slippery like tiles – lots of purchase for the feet) and exposed wooden beams, it looked like it might as well have had a ladder propped up against it.

She stuffed the stone she'd used to draw the X into her bag and, with a grin, she gripped the protruding part of the nearest beam and pulled herself up the wall, grabbing on to the edge of the thatch and swinging herself up onto the roof before she could lose momentum. She had to scramble around in a circle to orient herself, but before she could spot the telephone wire and the runners that were hanging from it, she spotted something even stranger: a graffiti tag that had apparently been spray-painted onto the thatch. It was quite a good graffiti tag too, not one of those blocky monstrosities that might as well have said 'I WAS HERE', but an elegant multicoloured design in letters that were almost too pretty to be legible. After a bit of squinting and some redrawing of the relevant bits of the tag in her notebook, Julie came to the conclusion that the tag said 'PIJONZ', which meant nothing to her, and so she turned back around to see if she could get a good shot at the runners with the stone.

There was a pigeon sitting on the line. Julie frowned. 'Shoo!' she said, flapping her hands in the pigeon's direction. 'Get off!'

The pigeon turned its head slowly round to face Julie. 'Are you talking to me?' it said.

'You *what*?'

The pigeon shuffled awkwardly along the telephone line. 'Cos there's no one else here,' it said. 'Are you talking to *me*?'

'I'm not sure –'

'Are you a spy?' the pigeon said, interrupting her. 'You don't look like a spy, but then again, a spy that looked like a spy wouldn't be a very good spy. Well? Are you?'

'I'm not a spy! Why would you even –' She stopped herself from finishing that sentence. There were plenty of reasons for anyone in the City to think that anyone else in the City was a spy, and just at that moment she couldn't think why pigeons should be exempt from the general paranoia. 'Look,' she said firmly, 'I just want to get a closer look at those runners.'

'Do you, now?' said the pigeon, cocking its head to one side. 'And what's it worth to you?'

'Oh, for the love of – are you going to charge me? Is that it? You want me to bribe you to fly away from that wire?'

The pigeon puffed up its chest and shuffled back and forth in an affronted sort of way. 'A bribe, is it? Is that what you think of the pigeon race? That we'll do anything for a few breadcrumbs?'

'I never said –'

'Seagull propaganda, that's what it is!'

'What are you –'

'Now, I'm a kind-hearted bird, anyone round here'll tell you that, but when it comes to seagulls –' The pigeon cooed suddenly and wriggled a little, and on the street below there was a moist *splat* sound. '*That's* what I think of seagulls. Dirty lying feckers, the lot of them. Are you with the seagull patrol?' it added abruptly.

Julie sighed. 'Look, a spy might not always look like a spy, but I'm pretty sure a seagull always looks like a seagull.'

The pigeon laughed. 'Shows what you know, miss. Shows what you know.'

'In any case, can I see the runners?'

'I don't know. How's your eyesight?'

'I meant, can I get them? I need to look at them more closely.'

The pigeon shuffled closer, one step, two steps, three, then abandoned the shuffle and flew the short distance between the runners and Julie's feet. It looked up at her with a distinctly suspicious air. 'You don't look like a seagull,' it said. 'You don't smell like a seagull. But you can't always tell. Seagulls are cunning little feckers.'

'Look, I'm not – how can I prove to you that I'm not a seagull? Wait –' She pulled down the shoulder of her top. 'Look, here. See those marks? I got arrested last night. I was carried to the Tower of Light by a seagull patrol. Doesn't that prove that I'm not a seagull? I don't even *like* seagulls. Got no reason to.'

The pigeon fluttered its wings and flew up to perch on Julie's head, peering down at her shoulder. Its claws dug into her scalp painfully and, now that it was so close, she was unpleasantly aware that its plumage was none too clean. And what on earth had it been eating to have breath that smelled like that?

To her relief, the pigeon fluttered down again a moment later. 'Good enough,' it said. 'You're not a seagull. Now, what do you want the runners for?'

'What? Now you want an explanation?'

The pigeon puffed up its chest again. 'Look, I don't think you're aware of where you are, young miss. This here's pigeon territory, see?' It pointed a wing at the tag painted on the roof. 'Not just this house, but the street, and not just the street but this whole quarter. Us pigeons rule the roost here, and nothing happens without our say-so!'

'And are you at war with the seagulls?'

'We've always been at war with them cockle-sucking feckers. Only, since the queen started losing her marbles, it's been ten times worse, seeing as now they're a *special patrol*.' The pigeon started shuffling back and forth on the roof, as if it were pacing; Julie noticed that one of its claws was badly deformed, so that it could only hobble. 'They put on airs like you wouldn't feckin' believe these days, but they don't patrol the pigeon territories, oh no! They'd get mobbed if they tried.'

Julie perked up. 'Really?'

'Would I lie to you?'

'And is this area the whole of the pigeon territories?'

'No, no – the Viking quarter's ours too.' Julie started at the thought of the City having a Viking quarter, but the pigeon didn't seem to notice. 'And some bits of the Liberties, but they're not, what d'you call it … secure. We're still fighting over them.'

'So … if you're at war with the seagulls, you must not be too friendly with the queen?'

The pigeon stopped pacing and stared at her. 'What have kings and queens to do with birds?'

It seemed to be a genuine question, and Julie was at a loss to answer it. 'Well … I … I don't know.'

The pigeon nodded. 'Us neither, and that's why this business with the seagulls is such a head-wrecker. It's not natural! Toadying up to Her Nibs like that, as if she had anything to do with the life of a bird. Eat your grub, find your mate, make your nest, lay your eggs, feed your squabs. That's us. That's the pigeons. It should be the seagulls too, only they've got corrupted.'

Julie pondered this. It would probably be rude to point out that spray-painting tags on rooftops and controlling territories in cities and, for that matter, talking to humans in their own language didn't normally have anything to do with the life of a bird, either, and even though she was rather curious to see whether the pigeon was aware of this, and what it meant by 'corruption', she was also anxious to find Molly Red before Aisling could get too far away, and she suspected that this particular pigeon would be a frustrating person to have an argument with.

'Do you know Molly Red?' she said.

'I know *of* her,' said the pigeon cautiously. 'Why do you ask?'

'I think those runners are a message for me from Molly Red,' she said. She took a deep breath. In the wrong company, what she was about to say would be dangerous, but if there really weren't any seagulls around, she should be safe. 'I want to help her overthrow the queen. If the queen falls, the seagulls won't be her guards any more, and that'll help the pigeons. So, really, it's in your own interests to help me get those runners.'

The pigeon looked at her consideringly for a

moment, then it hopped a little closer. 'you're going to overthrow the queen, are you?'

'Well, not on my own –'

'You and what army, then?'

'I don't have an army,' she said. 'Maybe Molly Red does; I don't know. But I swore I'd find a way to get the Queen-that-was out of her cage – to kill her properly, so she could come back again. I swore it. And I swore that I would leave the City of the Three Castles with a better ruler than it had when I came here.'

The pigeon chuckled. 'You've got something, young one,' it said, sounding impressed. 'Not sure what it is – maybe it's courage, maybe stupidity. Hard to tell the difference sometimes. But it's not enough. Pigeons don't do favours for nobody.'

'But I just *said* it would be in your interests –'

'*If* what you say is right, and *if* Molly Red has a hope in all the Realms Between of succeeding. Which I say she hasn't. Somebody else might, but you haven't mentioned somebody else, so that's by the by. So. A favour for a favour. *Comprende?*'

Julie sighed. 'What kind of favour?'

'Oh, well, it's a small enough thing you're asking, so … next time you see a seagull, throw a stone at it.'

Julie thought of the seagulls that had carried her to the Tower of Light, their sharp, piercing cries, so loud and high they were painful to hear, their talons digging into her ankles and her shoulders; she thought of how scared Aisling had been, so scared she could barely breathe. She thought of the stone she still had in her bag, ready to be used for marking another wall if that turned out to be necessary.

I can always miss on purpose, she thought. 'All right,' she said. 'I'll do it.' For the third time, she felt the promise settling on her scalp and tightening slightly. It made her wonder whether there was a limit on the number of oaths a person could be subject to at one time. Did the feeling get tighter the harder the promise would be to fulfil?

The pigeon nodded solemnly. 'Fair's fair,' it said, and flew the short distance to the middle of the telephone wire, where it picked up the runners by the laces and flew back again, dropping them at Julie's feet. 'That's my end of the bargain. Now you – ah, bejasus! Feckin' seagulls!'

It took off into the air in a flurry of wings. Julie looked up instinctively, only realising afterwards that that was probably a bad idea. Despite the pigeon's proud claim that there were no seagull patrols in pigeon territory, there was a flock of seagulls wheeling overhead, silent except for the beat of their wings. In a dreamy sort of way, she was aware of opening her bag and digging inside it for the stone. She seemed to have lost control of her hands; she certainly wasn't telling them to do what they were doing. With the part of her mind that was thinking, she was aware that it would be a bad idea to throw a stone at a seagull *now*. Those seagulls must have been sent after her by the queen, with sterner orders than usual, since they were venturing into the territory of rival birds. Indeed, Julie could see a flock – or rather, since they were nothing like as coordinated as the seagulls, a messy and disorganised rabble – of pigeons shooting up from the rooftops in the surrounding streets and hurling themselves through the sky at the seagulls. Julie wished she could look at them properly; as it was, she could only see them dimly in her peripheral vision. She had lost control of her eyes as well: they were determinedly focused on one seagull in particular, a seagull that seemed to be leading the flock, or at least was always the first to move.

It was the first one I saw, she thought, with the part of her mind that was conscious. *That's why –*

The leading seagull flew ahead suddenly, giving her a clear shot, and without being able to stop herself or aim wide or give it anything but her best possible try, she flung the stone at it and hit it squarely on the head.

She couldn't hear the sound the stone made as it connected with the seagull's head, nor the sound the seagull's body made when it fell to the ground. She stayed rooted where she was while the flock of gulls lost its pattern for a moment and then regrouped around a new leader, which gave a long cry and led the remaining gulls away from the pigeons, who turned in the air and followed as their enemies retreated.

Before the pigeon – any of the pigeons – could come back and talk to her, she picked up the runners, slung them over her shoulder by the laces, and ran down along the roof of the house she was on. She leapt more with abandon than confidence onto the next roof, and then the next, and the next, until she reached a roof that sloped low enough that she felt she could jump down without breaking a leg. She tucked herself under the eaves, in a corner that she was pretty sure hadn't been there five minutes ago, and sank down to a crouch, hugging her knees to her chest.

It'll just come back, she thought. *It'll come back in a different form. It's not really properly dead.*

It didn't help. But brooding didn't help either. She took a deep breath and let go of her legs, rearranging them into a more comfortable position, and unslung the runners from her shoulder. Now that she had them in her hand, she could see that the linings were red as well as the laces; a nice touch. They were good runners, stylish and comfortable-looking. They looked like they were her size too.

She felt around inside them both and pulled out the piece of paper she'd seen sticking out of the left one. It was soft and slightly damp; she wrinkled her nose at the thought that Molly Red, or whoever, had been wearing the shoes and had stuffed the note underneath their feet. At least it didn't smell.

She unfolded the note and read the slightly blurry letters:

Hello there, friend of the pigeons. I know what you're thinking. Yes, these shoes once belonged to Molly Red. But you can take them if you like. She doesn't need them any more.

Julie looked at the runners consideringly, then at her thin-soled ballet slippers. They weren't meant to be walked in, not as much as she'd been doing, and they certainly hadn't been designed for climbing and running along rooftops. She tucked the note under her armpit and untied the knot in the laces, slipping the runners onto her feet as soon as she'd untangled it. They were wonderfully soft and comfortable, even without socks, and she sighed with relief as she laced them up. That would make things much easier.

She tucked her shoes into her bag – they just about fitted – and resumed reading the note.

Come to the Viking quarter if you want to meet the one who used to wear these shoes.

Julie looked up from the note. 'Who would be stupid enough to do that?' she wondered out loud. 'It's obviously a trap.'

You're probably thinking that this is a trap, the note went on. *And you're right. But is a trap that you walk into willingly and knowingly really a trap?*

'Yes,' said Julie. 'Now you're just nitpicking.'

Nitpicking aside, the note continued, *if you're not a friend of She Whose Title We Will Not Mention Because It Only Encourages Her, the trap will be humane, and you will not be harmed or imprisoned for longer than it takes for me to be sure you're on the level. This I swear by the blood in which I have signed my name below. Yours in solidarity, Molly Red.*

The name was written in a rather shakier hand than the rest of the note, and where the rest of it had been in plain black ink, the signature was a blotchy, faded reddish-brown. Julie held the note up close to her eyes and peered at it. It *could* have been blood. It probably was. There was no way to be sure, but it seemed plausible.

The Viking quarter, then. The pigeons could tell her where it was. She got up, dusted herself off and tucked the note into her bag, just in case she needed it later. It wouldn't prove she was against the queen, but it might be useful to show why she'd come.

She looked up and down the narrow, twisty little street she'd found herself in. There was no sign of a pigeon anywhere; the local birds must have been off harrying the seagulls still. Julie shouldered her bag and walked off in a random direction, keeping an eye on the roofs and the sky in case a pigeon flew by overhead. She kept count of the corners she turned and crossroads she came to, and when she'd been past three crossroads and turned around five corners without seeing a pigeon, she decided to change her tactics: rather than walking around streets she was pretty sure were changing behind her back anyway, she'd stay still in one place and wait for the pigeons to come there.

She walked a short way down the street, until she found a place where the hard-packed earth was white with pigeon droppings, and settled in to wait.

It didn't take long before she got bored and started rummaging through her bag for something to occupy her mind; she considered flipping through her notebook and reading old entries, but a wave of homesickness came over her when she pulled it out. She had some games on her phone but none that she particularly liked playing; but while she was putting it back into the bag, her fingers bumped up against another phone, one she'd forgotten she had.

Aisling's phone was stylish and expensive, a more advanced model than hers. Despite the telephone wires running from house to house, she had not seen hide nor hair of a telephone or anything similar in all the time she'd spent in the City; she suspected that the wires were not really telephone wires so much as convenient perches for the pigeons (and probably also for the seagulls, in other parts of the City). Still, she took Aisling's phone out and took a look at it. Sure enough, it couldn't pick up a signal, and once Julie'd figured out how to use it, there was a lot of stuff on it that either didn't work without a connection or that probably worked pretty well but that she wasn't interested in.

Then there were the things she *was* interested in and probably shouldn't be. Was it all right to look at Aisling's call history? Probably not, but Julie couldn't resist – only to find that Aisling seemed to get and make a lot of calls to people who weren't in her contacts list and came up as unlabelled strings of numbers. Disappointed, Julie took a look in her photo album, hoping for shots of Aisling with her weirdo mates, drunk and acting silly, or just acting silly. But there were no party pictures there, only shots of odd-looking graffiti, a picture of what looked like the beach at Sandycove on a bright, clear day, a street performer in an outlandish costume, and (most puzzling of all) a shot of Julie herself, in her PE uniform, bullying-off at the beginning of a hockey match. She recognised the girl from the opposing team; the picture must have been old, since the game had taken place in the previous season. Julie had barely been aware of Aisling's existence back then.

She turned to Aisling's text messages, swearing to herself that this was absolutely her *last* invasion of Aisling's privacy and she would never, ever do it again. The inbox was full of messages that were impeccably spelled but still cryptic enough that even if they'd revealed Aisling's secrets Julie wouldn't have learned anything from them, apart from the fact that Aisling's friends used proper spelling even in text messages (which Julie thought was a waste of effort). She was about to put the phone away when she noticed that there was an undelivered message in the outbox that had been saved at 9.13 pm, and that had a very familiar number attached to it.

Why would Aisling have been trying to text her?

She checked the message with shaking fingers.

Julie: escaping w/ rabbit who wants my help. If you get out, go where we 1st arrived to City. I'll be there or leave a message. Love & hugs A

Julie bit her lip. If she had seen the message before – if she had thought to *look* for the message … But what did it change, after all? She was lost in a warren of streets and houses that were so unfamiliar and unpredictable that there was no point in trying to find her way out. She had no idea where the quays were in relation to where she was now, and no way of getting there even if she had. No, it changed nothing: she would still have to go to the Viking quarter and meet Molly Red there, and maybe (if she was lucky) Molly Red would help her find Aisling.

She stuffed the phone back into her bag and looked up, scanning the roofs and the overhead wires for pigeons, her arms wrapped around her chest.

Actually, it wasn't completely true that the note didn't change anything. It didn't change what she had to do, that was certain, but now she knew that Aisling was – well, not that she was all right, because who knew what a rabbit might really be in a place like this; but she had escaped and gone with the rabbit of her own free will, and it was better to know that than to know only that she wasn't in a cell. And when Julie had thought that over, she was able to admit to herself that it made her feel better that Aisling had been considerate enough to leave a note.

That was a thought she didn't want to examine too much.

'Where are those stupid pigeons, anyway?' she muttered to herself, pacing back and forth. 'Just like Dublin Bus, you are. Or taxis. Or in-service training days for teachers. Never there when you're wanted, all over the place when you're not. How am I supposed to get to the Viking quarter now?'

The sides of her bag started to bulge, as if of their own accord, and something inside seemed to be rustling. Puzzled, she unzipped it, and the note from Molly Red snaked out of the bag and into her hand, where it lay inert, just a normal piece of paper again. She unfolded it and read, at the bottom of the note, underneath what she had already read, in a space she was completely certain had been blank before:

If you needed directions to the Viking quarter, you should have asked. I'm not psychic, you know.

'Wha – ? Are you … is this paper … are you listening to me?'

Words started appearing on the paper, as if they were being written down by an invisible hand.

Not listening, exactly, but this paper has a limited ability to respond to spoken questions. Now, ask me nicely and I'll tell you how to get to the Viking quarter from where you are.

'You want me to ask nicely? That's rich! Why should I be polite? You're only a piece of paper!'

The note instantly folded itself up into a snap-dragon shape, like one of the paper fortunetellers she used to make in boring classes in primary school, and folded a part of itself up and into the mouth of the snap-dragon to make a sticking-out tongue. It didn't actually make a raspberry noise, which would have been hard to do with paper, but the rustling sound it made with its 'lips' had a similar tone of rude contempt.

'Now you're just being childish,' said Julie when it had re-unfolded itself and settled back as a flat piece of paper. 'Look, I don't owe you anything, you or the person who made you. I don't see any reason to be polite. You obviously want me to go to the Viking quarter, so why don't you just take me there and stop this faffing about?'

The note shifted around a little on her palm before the next message appeared. *Fine*, it said. *But don't say I didn't warn you.*

At that, the note slid up her wrist and arm and down her chest to slip back into her bag, and the tickling sensation was strange enough that for a moment she didn't notice that the laces of her shoes were untying and re-tying themselves, though by the time she had noticed that, and noticed the peculiarly-shaped knots the laces were taking, she had figured out what was going to happen next. Which didn't make it any less stomach-churningly disorienting when her shoes lifted up off the ground, one after the other, and walked her through the narrow winding streets as if she were being pulled around by magnets buried under the ground.

She had once done an exercise in PE class where the teacher had told one girl to lie down and follow the instructions of another girl exactly. The aim was only to get the girl who was lying down to stand up, but nobody was able to manage it, even though the whole class had a turn. 'You see how complicated your bodies are?' the teacher had said. 'You see how much you take them for granted?' This was like that: like her body was being ordered around by somebody who was vastly underestimating how complicated a human body was, somebody who thought that all you needed to do to make it walk was to move the feet. And so her feet would move, and the rest of her body would be jerked out of balance, and if she shifted to compensate, she'd be a second or two too slow for the next motion.

Her centre of gravity was always slightly off, and the up-and-down-ness of it made her seasick.

She was quite grateful when the shoes finally stopped, in among a cluster of thatched houses arranged around a market square that did, indeed, look Viking. Much to her surprise, there were people walking around, talking, working, moving from place to place; the rest of the City had felt more or less deserted, and the relief she felt now made her realise that that emptiness had been making her edgy and nervous ever since she had arrived. Though the people walking around looked as much like museum exhibits as people: rosy-cheeked men and women with long, braided hair the colour of wheat-stalks, the men sporting vast moustaches, all of them wearing belted tunics made of handspun wool, the market they were trading in the kind with open barrows of pigs' heads and apples rather than home-baked muffins and hygienically arranged tubs of olives and artichoke hearts.

Julie grabbed the arm of the first friendly-looking person who passed nearby her, a woman carrying a bucket full of some kind of fish. 'Hey,' she said, 'do you know Molly Red?'

The woman looked at her with a puzzled expression, said something Swedish-sounding that Julie couldn't understand, and pulled her arm away, sidestepping her neatly and walking on.

Julie sighed and let her head sink. Of course:

they didn't speak English. Not in Viking times. The Vikings would speak … she wasn't sure, Old Norse or something, probably, but the Irish …

Her head snapped up, and she turned around, calling out to the woman, '*Gabh mo leithscéal, an féidir leat cabhrú liom?*' She needed help, and there was no harm in being polite about it.

The woman turned around, looking even more puzzled than before. '*B'fhéidir,*' she said. (Her accent was strange, but Julie had heard worse in the Junior Cert aural exams.) '*An bhfuil tú ar strae?*'

That was a tricky one. Was she lost? Yes, of course; and no, not really. '*Níl, níl. Tá mé ceart go leor. Ach tá mé ag, ag –*' Damn, now she couldn't remember how to say 'looking for'. Did it begin with a C? No, an L – '*ag lorg bean arbh ainm di Molly Red. An bhfuil aithne agat uirthi?*'

'*Ó, tá!*' said the woman with a nod. '*Fan nóiméad, a chailín.*'

Julie smiled to show she was happy to wait, and the woman bustled away, neglecting her bucket a little in her haste. A fish slipped out of it, and a white cat squirmed out from under a market-trader's barrow and pounced on it, attacking the fish's eyes with such gusto that Julie felt her stomach churning again. And yet, now that she looked around, the market seemed a bit sanitised. The butcher's stall was close enough that she should have been able to smell the meat – there was

153

certainly enough of it – and yet all she could smell was a sweetish scent of hay, wholesome and pleasant. The people seemed a trifle too photogenic to be real too. She couldn't tell whether any of them had black teeth, but none of them looked pox-ridden or malnourished, and they all had well-tended hair and very good skin, which wasn't even normal in the twenty-first century, much less the tenth.

It's like a film set, she thought. *This isn't the real Viking Dublin. It's the PG version. The theme-park version. I bet somewhere in their houses, all these men have helmets with horns on, even though that's been proved to be a myth. It makes a pretty picture, and that's what people remember. And this place must be all made out of memories.*

'A chailín?'

She spun round, smiling, and followed the fish-woman into a cottage with a low door and no windows. The interior was dim, lit only by a turf fire and a few chinks in the thatched roof. It took Julie's eyes a moment to adjust, and when they did, she wasn't sure she was seeing what she thought she was seeing: a woman sitting by the fire, wrapped up in a deer's hide, who had the exact same face as the queen. Not the same hair – this woman's hair was long, hanging in thick shiny locks down her back and on either side of her face – and her features were softened by an expression much kinder and gentler than the queen had had for the short time Julie had seen her.

Julie cleared her throat. 'Are you Molly Red?' she said.

The woman frowned, and Julie shivered a little, though the cottage was, if anything, too warm. When she frowned, this woman looked almost exactly like the queen.

'No,' said the woman, 'I am not Molly Red, though she's served me in the past and no doubt will do again. I suppose you're a friend of the pigeons? She'll be around soon, don't worry.'

The woman looked away from Julie then, staring into the fire as if it held the secrets to all of life's mysteries. Julie sat down opposite her, cross-legged, and said a little tentatively, 'If you don't mind my asking, who are you?'

'Who do I look like?' said the woman, not shifting her gaze from the fire.

'You look like the queen. But you're not her. She's only got one eye, and she's in the Tower.'

The woman stared at her, her eyes as sharp and steely as the eye of the queen in the Tower. 'Indeed,' she said.

'You can't be the Queen-that-was, either, because she's in a cage.'

'That she is,' said the woman, nodding.

Julie felt her eyes going wide. 'Then – you're the Queen-that-will-be?'

The woman smiled. 'You are wise,' she said. 'And you

are searching for Molly Red? Beware: you shouldn't search for her unless you want her to find you.'

'Oh, I want her to find me! As far as I can tell, she's my best bet to get home. I mean, she's supposed to be someone who can stand against the queen – I mean, the Queen-that-is. The one-eyed queen. I swore I'd leave the City with a better ruler than it had when I arrived, and it seems like Molly Red's the one to do that. So …'

Julie trailed off. The woman had a triumphant glint in her eyes. Julie shivered; now she looked exactly like the one-eyed queen.

'Marvellous,' said the mysterious queen. 'You and Molly Red have both done well.'

That was supposed to be praise, Julie knew, so it was strange that it felt more like a threat.

Before Aisling had even finished shaking Molly Red's hand, Molly Red was looking around them and gesturing that they should leave the alleyway. Aisling followed her out into the open streets, her heart pounding. 'You didn't leave, then?' she said. 'They said you left. I mean, Jo Maxi and his friends. They said you must have left for mortal lands.'

'Don't believe everything you hear,' said Molly Red, 'especially in the Realms Between. Even people who don't tell lies can make mistakes, and what you tell them may not be what they hear.'

'But the horse – was that you?'

'The white horse with the red mane?' Molly Red tugged at her hair and smiled ironically. 'Of course it was me. And that means it's my fault you and your friend are here, and I'm sorry for that. I had the Queen-that-will-be on my back and the mad queen's hounds chasing me. Well, since I brought you here, I'll bring you back, or find you a way to go back by yourselves. Though that's easier said than done now that the gates are closed.'

She sniffed the air experimentally and then, without so much as a twitch for a warning, transformed into a white dog with red ears and a red tail. As a dog, she was large and bulky looking, the kind of dog that takes its owner for a walk rather than the other way around. She sniffed the air again, several times, then transformed back. 'Yes, this is the place,' she said. 'We need to obscure the scent. Do you have anything strong-smelling?'

'Give me a minute.' Aisling fumbled in the pockets of her coat. It had a lot of pockets, which was one of the reasons why she loved it, and in those pockets she had tucked away a lot of things that might prove useful: lipbalm; tissues; a multitool that might actually have been illegal, since the longest blade was pretty long (though she figured if she didn't take it out in public she wouldn't get into trouble); a spare pair of headphones that were smaller than her usual pair and not as good; wet wipes; a tiny little pad with a pencil attached and a packet of clove cigarettes she had bought in Paris and brought back to show to Darren.

'Here,' she said, proffering the packet. 'These things

stink. And they're even worse for you than normal cigarettes. They're a goth thing, you know, a sort of a ... Not that I've ever smoked, I just got them out of curiosity, really, after I read they'd been banned in America because supposedly they encourage ...'

She trailed off. *Oh, stop babbling*, she thought furiously at herself, watching Molly Red turn the packet over and over in her hand and lift it to her nose to sniff it. When she finally smiled, Aisling felt glorious relief.

'Perfect,' said Molly Red. She took one cigarette from the packet and held it aloft, staring at it with a frown of concentration. The tip of the cigarette burst into flame, then died down to a steady smoulder. 'Now, we need to obscure the trail of the gate and lay a false trail, or else the queen can find it and close it for good, and then we'll be in trouble.'

'You mean the Wormwood Gate?' Aisling said, following her as she walked in the opposite direction from how she and Julie had travelled when they first arrived.

'That's right,' said Molly Red.

'Um.' Something was nagging at Aisling, though she couldn't figure out what. 'Is it ... why does the queen want the gates closed?'

'Defence. Open gates means open travel, which means spies and enemies in the City that she can't control.'

That wasn't it.

'And why are you against that? I mean, I guess if the Wormwood Gate is closed, me and Julie will be stuck here, but apart from that, what harm will it do to close the Wormwood Gate?'

Molly Red stopped dead in front of Aisling, so that Aisling almost bumped into her. She wheeled around, wafting a cloud of sickly-sweet smoke into Aisling's face. Aisling coughed but stood her ground.

'I'm just asking,' she said. 'I'm a newbie; I don't know how this place works.'

Molly Red waved the cigarette in the air a little. 'This place is in the Realms Between,' she said, as if that were an answer, and when Aisling shrugged in bafflement, went on, 'which means that it's halfway between dreams and reality, between the kingdoms of Faerie and the lands of mortals. It's neither one thing nor the other, and it won't survive if it's cut off from either the paths that lead to Faerie lands or the gates that lead to mortal lands. It's like … a hammock, hanging between two trees. Cut down either of the ropes holding it up and it won't be anyone's bed any more. Just a sad little scrap of cloth.'

'I see,' said Aisling, and she thought she did, for once. 'But why does the queen want to close the Wormwood Gate if that'll kill the City? Doesn't she realise how dangerous that would be?'

Molly Red gave her a look – a long, assessing sort

of look. Aisling felt the urge to fidget or strike a pose; she resisted.

'There are those who would rather die than be conquered,' Molly Red said at last. 'And then there are those who would rather bleed to death than admit that making a gown out of knives was a foolish plan.'

'Pride?' said Aisling. 'That's all?'

'It's enough,' said Molly Red.

She pivoted again and strode away, and Aisling had let her go a dozen strides, wrapped up in her thoughts, before she called out, 'Wait! I've remembered something.' Molly Red turned and raised her eyebrows. 'I have to leave a message for my friend,' said Aisling. 'I promised I'd leave one in the place where we first came into the City, which is where the Wormwood Gate opened for us.'

'All right,' said Molly Red, trotting over to join her, 'but be quick about it.'

Aisling took out her pad and pencil and started scribbling a note.

Dear Julie,

It turns out the rabbit who rescued me was Molly Red all along! I wish I could say I wasn't surprised, but I'm not that used to this place yet. I keep expecting it to make sense and it never does. It always …

Aisling stopped writing and shook her head. No. Too

rambly. She tore out the page and started again.

Dear Julie,

The rabbit who broke me out of our cell was Molly Red in disguise. Yes, turns out those three guys were misinformed: she's alive and in the City, and trying to thwart the queen. I'm going with her to help muffle the trail of the Wormwood Gate. I don't really understand what's going on, but I figure the enemy of our enemy is our friend, more or less, and the queen is definitely our enemy.

I hope you're all right. If you're reading this I suppose you must be. I wish you were here. I really liked being with you and I wish …

She stopped. Too mushy. Another page.

Julie,

The rabbit was Molly Red. She's alive and in the City and I'm helping her, for now, because she's trying to thwart the queen and the queen is obviously evil. If you can smell clove cigarettes, follow that smell; that's where we've been. I'm all right, and I hope you are too. Good luck. See you soon.

Aisling

She hesitated and looked around. There wasn't really anywhere prominent to put the message. She could stuff it into a crack between two bricks or cobblestones, but Julie probably wouldn't see it unless she searched the whole street, and that would waste a lot of time.

Molly Red was shifting from foot to foot, swinging her arms; it was such an ostentatious display of impatience that Aisling suspected she wasn't really *that* impatient, and so she took her time to think of a way of making the message stand out. Eventually, she took out her multitool, prised out the longest blade, and slid it across the cobblestones in a sweeping capital J, three feet long, followed by a U, an L, an I and an E. She folded the message, emptied the packet of tissues, put the message into the packet, stuffed the packet into a crack between two stones underneath the big JULIE, and carved arrows pointing towards the correct crack.

'There,' she said to Molly Red, after waiting another few seconds, just to be contrary. 'Now we can go.'

Molly Red said nothing, only nodded and took off in a slightly different direction than they'd gone before.

They had been walking in total silence (Molly Red taking out a new cigarette each time the old one had nearly burned down to the filter) for what felt like five minutes when Aisling finally said, 'What are you going to do next? I mean, once we've muffled the trail. What's the next step?'

Molly Red picked up the cigarette and started walking again. 'I can't tell you that,' she said.

'Oh, *what*?' said Aisling, but she didn't stop walking, though she wanted to. 'Why not?'

'You've heard it said that walls have ears?'

Aisling nodded.

'Well, in the City of the Three Castles, the sky has ears too.'

She tipped her head back as she spoke, and Aisling followed her eyes to see seagulls wheeling overhead.

'I see,' she said, looking down unhappily. 'Then I suppose it's not your fault.'

They walked in silence for a few more steps before Molly Red said quietly, 'You're not from around here. Can you keep a secret?'

'Of course,' said Aisling.

Molly Red leaned close so that her lips were barely a centimetre away from Aisling's ear.

'It *is* my fault,' she whispered. 'All of this is my fault. That's why I'm trying to put things right.'

She pulled back, and Aisling stared at her. Her expression was bright and unconcerned; they might have been talking about the weather. 'Well,' said Aisling, 'I mean. Um. When you say –'

Behind them there was a clatter of hooves, and Aisling spun round, reaching into her pocket for the multitool. There was a huge chestnut mare with a shaggy mane and a wild look in her eyes barrelling towards them, and her rider seemed to be having trouble controlling her.

Aisling shifted the multitool to her left hand and reached forward with her right, walking slowly towards the horse.

'Shh, now,' she said, and made a clicking noise with her tongue. 'Easy. Easy.'

The horse reared up on her hind legs with a frightened-sounding whinny, but Aisling stood her ground, still clicking. 'Easy, easy. It's all right, girl. Nothing to fear here. We're all friends now, hm?'

The horse turned around in a circle once, twice, three times, and shoved her head so close to Aisling's that Aisling could smell her breath. Then, finally, the horse shook her mane and seemed to calm down. Aisling patted the horse's nose with a cautious hand. 'There, now,' she murmured, 'nothing to worry about, see?'

'You have a way with horses,' said the rider. Aisling had only registered at first that he was a tall man with long hair in a ponytail. Now that the horse was standing more or less still and she could get a better look, she could see that he had a beard and was wearing a fine white shirt with puffy sleeves and a waistcoat made of leather with an intricate lace-like pattern carved into it. No helmet (not that she would have expected a rider in this bizarre place to understand basic safety protocols), and the riding breeches and boots he wore looked easily two hundred years out of fashion.

He spoke with an odd accent too: sort of English

sounding, but not quite. 'I ride every weekend,' Aisling said, stroking the mare's head from between her ears to the tip of her nose. 'If you'll forgive my bluntness, who might you be? There aren't many people out and about in the City, between one thing and another.'

The man looked at her, looked at Molly Red, then looked into the middle distance as if he were making some kind of calculation, and finally dismounted – rather elegantly, considering how huge his horse was. He handed the reins to Aisling and bowed to her and Molly Red.

'I am Morgan de Meath,' he said, 'Count Palatine of the Realms Between. I offer you my true name in token of the power bestowed upon me by the kings and queens of the Seven Free Kingdoms of the Fae. I care for the Realms on their behalf.'

Molly Red gave a loud and obviously fake cough. 'And what might you be doing with yourself in this city?' she said.

'I am on a mission from her majesty the Queen of Crows,' he said. 'Please, I cannot offer you anything in exchange for your assistance, apart from my gratitude, but may I ask if either of you is known as Molly Red?'

Now it was Aisling's turn to cover up laughter with a fake cough. She looked at Molly Red, eyebrows raised, trying to ask without using words whether she could tell him that he'd found the person he was looking for; that, yes, as it turned out, the one called 'Molly Red' was, in fact, the one with the bright scarlet hair, not the brunette in the leather coat.

Molly Red didn't seem to pick up her meaning. She grabbed the reins from Aisling's hand and yanked them, which the mare didn't like at all; she let out an indignant neigh and jerked her head back.

'Don't say names so freely, your own or anyone else's!' she said. 'And don't expect to find any help here. This is not a city of friends and allies – not any more; not since that one-eyed lunatic became queen.'

'I followed the scent of cloves, as it was written in the letter,' said the count, not seeming to notice his horse's distress. 'Was that a lying letter, then?'

'That letter wasn't meant for you!' said Aisling. 'Did you at least leave it behind for Julie?'

Abashed, the count shook his head. 'I was sent on a mission of utmost urgency,' he said apologetically. 'I have been here for many an hour, and I found no one to help me and no clue as to where I might find Molly Red, until I found that letter. I could wish I had not read it, were it not my only way of fulfilling my orders from the Queen of Crows.' He sighed and absent-mindedly reached out a hand to pat his horse's flank. The horse seemed to find his touch soothing, for she quieted down immediately. 'She delights in giving me orders I cannot obey. I thought – I hoped I could at least find Molly Red and offer her the assistance the Queen of Crows wants me to give.'

Molly Red let go of the reins and stood so that she was in between the count and his horse, with Aisling on her right side.

'And what kind of assistance did she tell you to offer me?'

The count's eyes flickered anxiously between Molly Red and Aisling. 'You are she, then?'

'That I am, though it may not profit you to have found me.'

He closed his eyes and sighed in relief, then opened them again. 'The precise words Her Majesty used were "whatever assistance she will accept",' he said, and Aisling thought she could see him leaning slightly towards Molly Red.

'*Really?*' said Molly Red, drawing the word out and tilting her head to one side, a speculative look in her eyes.

Aisling tasted bitterness in her mouth, and she swallowed, willing her stomach to stop doing somersaults and going crazy with the acid production. The last thing she needed was to get reflux on top of everything else that was happening.

'Yes,' said the count. 'You must know that, as a Fae, I cannot tell a lie.'

'*You* must know,' Molly Red countered, 'that not everyone in the Fae kingdoms is a Fae. And that we're not in the kingdoms now.'

The count dipped his head, conceding the point.

'Nevertheless, we are in the Realms Between, and the Realms Between are under the protection of the seven kingdoms, however nominal the authority of the kings and queens may be in practice. I could not have been dispatched otherwise.'

'You could have been dispatched on the whim of the Queen of Crows. She's not the type to care about jurisdiction when it doesn't suit her.'

The count shuffled his feet, his hand curling into a fist on the horse's flank. 'I cannot deny that. Yet I had it from her own mouth that I was to be sent on the basis of my authority – my supposed authority – as Count Palatine.'

'And she told you – what? "Go to the City of the Three Castles, find Molly Red, and offer her whatever assistance she will accept"?'

'Not in those words.'

'In what words, then?'

The count's eyes grew distant, and he spoke as if reciting from memory: '"I am sending you to a city that was once part of the Kingdom of Crows and is now in the Realms Between, under your authority. It is called the City of the Three Castles, and it has been thrown into turmoil. Go there and find the one known as Molly Red – that is her make-name, not her true name – and offer her whatever assistance she will accept."'

'I see,' said Molly Red. 'And you didn't ask her why?

You didn't ask her who I was that she was so eager to help me?'

The count looked at her as if she was mad. 'Question the Queen of Crows? The Queen of the Lands of Death? Her power is great, and her temper is legend. I would be a fool to think of such a thing.'

'Would you, now?' A corner of Molly Red's mouth quirked upwards in a lopsided smile.

The count raised his hands in surrender. 'This is all very well, but I was not sent to speak to you. I was sent to assist you. What assistance can I offer you that you will accept? Whatever it is, I am bound by my oath to the Queen of Crows to give it to you.'

'I'll have your horse, for starters.'

'Then she is yours.'

Molly Red nodded. 'Mount the horse,' she said with a jerk of her head, speaking to Aisling without looking at her.

Aisling obeyed, shifting the multitool from hand to hand as she did, not wanting to put it away; it was a comfort to have it ready. Once she had her feet in the stirrups and a good seat in the saddle, she pulled the longest blade out and held the tool ready with her left hand while her right held the reins. *Just in case*, she thought. *Probably nothing will happen.*

'Is there anything else I can offer you?' asked the count.

'If I asked you to break your oath to the Queen of

Crows and swear an oath to me instead – I suppose you couldn't do that?'

'Of course not.'

'Hmm.' Molly Red stepped in close to him and spoke so softly that Aisling had to lean over a little to hear what she said.

'I can tell you haven't heard what they say about me. Why the one-eyed queen is afraid of me. Did you know there's a rumour I swore an oath of fealty to the Queen of Crows and broke it when she gave me an order I didn't like?'

The count's eyes widened. 'Is that true?' he said in a shocked whisper.

Molly Red stepped back, smiling. 'It's true,' she said. 'They call me the Oathbreaker. They speak of me in whispers. They say I could tear down all seven of the Kingdoms if I wished it. Now tell me, O Count Palatine of the Realms Between, why would the Queen of Crows send you to help a person like me?'

'No doubt –' The count's voice croaked; he cleared his throat and started again. 'No doubt she has her reasons.'

'No doubt. Unless she doesn't know. Unless she believes I'm still loyal to her.'

The count's mouth opened and closed a few times. 'I don't know what you think you're doing,' he said, 'but I entreat you to stop and deal with me plainly.'

'I'm just pointing out that there are things I know

that your mistress hasn't told you. She didn't tell you I was her servant, did she?'

'No, Her Majesty never –'

'And I know things about you too. I'd wager she never told you that she stole you away from mortal lands as a child so that you could walk freely through all the kingdoms and the Realms Between to do her bidding. That your blood is not Fae, not even a little bit.'

The count shook his head slowly. He didn't seem to know how to react. Aisling squeezed the reins in her fist, distressed on his behalf.

Molly Red took another step back, until she was within reach of Aisling and the horse.

'I know more than I've told you,' Molly Red said to the count, 'and I'll tell you all of it one day, if you like. But today, I'll only tell you one more thing.'

With a movement so swift that Aisling could barely see it, she grabbed the multitool from Aisling's hand and lunged forward, thrusting the blade into the count's chest before he could react. He staggered backwards, clutching at the wound she had made, and fell onto the cobblestones, his mouth gaping.

'No, two more things,' said Molly Red calmly, wiping the blade on her sleeve. 'The first thing is: you are not as firmly bound to the Queen of Crows as you think. And the second thing is: if you bind yourself any more firmly, you'll lose your last ties to the mortal world, and then you'll never learn any more of the secrets she's been keeping from you.'

She folded the blade back into the multitool and swung herself up into the saddle behind Aisling, giving the horse's flanks a mighty kick. The horse whinnied and broke into a gallop before Aisling could react, carrying them over cobbles and tarmac and concrete, rushing and rushing through streets that flew by so fast Aisling could barely see them. Her mouth tasted of acid and her eyes were watering; Molly Red had grabbed onto her waist so tightly she felt bruised, and the horse was galloping so fast and so wildly that a sort of giddy panic set in, and then, to her surprise, faded away, leaving her feeling quite calm and strangely distant from what was going on.

I'm not seated securely, Aisling thought, *and I have no helmet, so the longer we keep up this speed the more likely it is that I'll fall, and if I do fall, there's a high chance I'll suffer a serious head injury. But I can't just yank the reins because this mare is a wild one and she'll rear, and then I'll fall for sure.*

Molly Red let go of her waist and put her hands over Aisling's, interrupting her thoughts. 'What are you doing?' Aisling cried, her words whipped away by the wind of their passage. 'Your feet aren't in the stirrups, you'll –'

'Beg your pardon,' Molly Red whispered into her ear, 'but I need the reins.'

She grabbed the reins just below where Aisling had a hold of them and pulled gently on the left one. The horse reared a little – enough to make Aisling's heart leap into her throat, but not enough to throw her to the ground – and veered off to the left, at a slightly slower gallop than before.

'Where are we going?' Aisling called out, biting her lip when she heard the tremor in her voice. 'Why did you do that?'

'Now's not the time for talk,' Molly Red whispered, again directly into Aisling's ear, and Aisling shivered without quite knowing why. She pulled on the reins – gently – and the horse slowed down to a very uncomfortable trot, until Molly Red gave the horse's flanks another kick, and she broke into a canter. That, at least, was a pace Aisling knew how to handle.

'Let go of the reins,' Aisling said. 'I'll steer her any way you want us to go, but you need to let me have the reins.'

'Very well,' said Molly Red, and she withdrew her hands from the reins and wrapped her arms around Aisling's waist again, which was not much more comfortable. Aisling slowed the horse to a trot, and when Molly Red didn't complain, slowed down further to a walk. Now that they weren't speeding along as fast and furious as a hurricane, she could untangle which feelings were coming from her and which from the way the horse was moving; her heart was taking much longer to slow down than the horse's hooves, and her breathing was coming out in shallow, laboured pants.

'Here,' said Molly Red at last, after a few minutes of increasingly slow walking. Aisling tugged on the reins one last time, and the horse stopped obediently. There was a stone horse-trough against the wall of a nearby building, and unlike the horse-troughs on Stephen's Green, this one was actually full of water. When they had both dismounted, Aisling led the horse to the trough, where it dunked its head in the water and drank greedily.

'Well,' said Aisling, leaning against the wall to spare her shaky legs, 'is *now* the time for talk?'

'Perhaps,' said Molly Red. 'Oh, by the way –' She took something out of the pocket of her hoodie and handed it to Aisling. Aisling stared at it, feeling number and blanker than she had ever felt.

It was the multitool, the little *no-not-a-Swiss-Army-knife-that's-a-different-brand* that she'd bought from Petersen's with her birthday money and carried around for six months without ever using it for more than cutting off a loose thread from a skirt. It was folded up now, and if she pulled out the longest of the blades, she was sure it would not have a trace of a stain on it. Molly Red had wiped it pretty carefully after she'd used it. Aisling could see the dark stain on her white sleeve.

'I feel sick,' she said faintly, and only now that she

had said it out loud did she realise it was true.

'Well, don't vomit into the trough,' said Molly Red, 'the horse is still drinking.'

'What is *wrong* with you?' Aisling blurted out, the words exploding from her like juice from an overripe tomato. 'You just killed a man!'

'He might not be dead,' said Molly Red. 'I didn't check.'

'But you want him to be dead! You stabbed him in the chest! I mean, I mean – even if you somehow miraculously managed to miss all the vital organs, it's pretty obvious that you had criminal intentions coming out your ears!'

Molly Red raised one eyebrow. 'You must know by now that death doesn't mean the same thing here as it does in mortal lands.'

'You told him *he* was a mortal!'

'I told him he had mortal blood, which is not the same thing. He's like me, you see. A Betweener. Born mortal, but … He's been in the Fae kingdoms so long, they've soaked into him. He'll pay the Ferryman's fee and come back with a new shape to shift into, the same way I do when I die.'

Aisling stared at her. She was perfectly relaxed and calm, even nonchalant, her hands in her pockets and her mouth quirked into a half-smile.

'Why did you kill him?' she said.

Molly Red glanced up at the sky, then looked down

again and said, 'Because he was a spy. Not that he knew it. But he was going to report back to the Queen of Crows because he was still loyal to her. He didn't know how she'd been lying to him. I had to send him to the Ferryman to prove to him that he – the Count – is more like me than than like the Queen of Crows.'

'But why –'

'He knows I have a tongue that can lie. I could tell him the truth until the sun fell from the sky, and he'd still not believe me. But there are three different ways across the River: one for mortals, one for the Fae, and one for those that are in between.'

'Like you?'

'Like me. And Morgan de Meath.'

Aisling closed her eyes and took a deep breath. When she opened them again, she was still there, with the horse and the trough and Molly Red with her hands in her pockets.

She walked over to the trough and dipped her hand in the water; it was cool, and she patted her face with it, then wiped the water off with her other hand.

'When you said it was your fault,' she said, 'what did you mean?'

Molly Red took her hands out of her pockets and walked over, leaning on the side of the trough and speaking quietly. 'I set the Queen-that-is and the Queen-that-was to quarrelling,' she said. 'Let slip a rumour here and a half-truth there, and let them think the Queen of Crows was planning to invade, but gave them different ideas about what to do.'

'And then they fought …?'

Molly Red nodded. 'And the mad one won the battle. That much I expected. The business with the cage, now – I didn't see that coming. She was a little madder than I had thought, you see. She wanted to change things, and she had a strong enough will to bend the rules, to take the throne before her time. That was enough to wake the Queen-that-was and bring her back from the lands of the dead. To keep the City from tearing itself apart from having three living queens in it, I had to take her away to mortal lands, let her cross the River and linger in the Ferryman's domain until it was safe for her to return.'

'And that's where Julie and I came in,' said Aisling. 'Literally, in fact. You were taking the Queen-that-was away when you knocked us over, right?'

'That I was. She should be by the banks of the River by now, if she hasn't crossed already.'

'Why did you do it? Make them fight, I mean. What's in it for you?'

Molly Red gave her a considering look. 'There are things I can't safely tell you,' she said at last, 'and that's one of them. I can tell you this much, and you can believe me or not, as it pleases you: my will is free and unbound and, in my heart, I am servant to no one. But in the eyes of the Queen of Crows, I am loyal to her and to the Kingdom of Crows. I'd like her to keep on thinking that. So when she gave me an order to rid the City of the Three Castles of its queens, I had to either make it look like I'd tried and failed or obey the order – in my own fashion.'

'Then the Queen of Crows really is invading the City?'

Molly Red laughed softly. 'The Queen of Crows doesn't give *that*' (she snapped her fingers) 'for the City – at least, not for its own sake. She just wants the queens gone because the queens have a treaty with the Lord of Shadows to let him move freely through the City, and her one desire in all the realms is to stop the Lord of Shadows from getting what he wants.' She shook her head sadly. 'It was a very messy divorce.'

'You mean the Lord of Shadows and the Queen of Crows were married?'

'For centuries, until it all went wrong. The years since their rupture have been … troubled, to say the least.'

'I can imagine,' said Aisling. Her parents were both lawyers, and they often dealt with divorce cases. 'This is … collateral damage?'

'That's one way of putting it. Though, mind you, there's more to it than that. They had plans, those two, to rule and conquer the Fae kingdoms and beyond, and now they're not together any more, they're each trying to outdo the other. They don't much care who

KATHERINE FARMAR

they crush in the attempt. But the Lord of Shadows is more subtle, so I don't know what his plan is.'

'Yet?'

Molly Red grinned, and Aisling felt a strange surge of pleasure. 'Yet,' Molly Red said, nodding.

An alarming thought occurred to Aisling. 'You said the count got to be a ... a Betweener because he stayed too long in Fae realms and ... something about cutting ties with mortal lands?'

'Yes. The Fae realms, the Realms Between ... they get under your skin, after a while. Become a part of you. That's how I got to be this way.'

'Then Julie and I shouldn't stay here too long.'

'Indeed you shouldn't. You've been here, what, a day? Less? That's safe enough, though there's no way of knowing how long is too long. Time doesn't always work here the way it seems to.'

Aisling felt her eyes widen. 'Oh,' she said. 'W-well. In that case, what's our next move?'

'Your friend has been looking for me,' said Molly Red. 'I think it's time I found her.'

8

Julie looked up as the door of the cottage opened and a woman walked in, her head bent at first to avoid hitting the lintel; she was dressed in white and her hair was a vivid scarlet.

The queen rose to her feet. 'So you have come, Molly Red!'

The red-haired woman nodded and stepped aside to make room for her companion. Julie stood up, stumbling slightly on a leg that had fallen asleep.

'Aisling!' Julie said and slapped her hand over her mouth. 'Um, I mean –'

'I know her name. As I know your name, Julie,' said the red-haired woman, looking at her in an assessing, calculating way that made Julie feel uncomfortable. She resisted the urge to look away or fidget, holding

Molly Red's gaze until she nodded and said, 'I see you found the shoes.'

'Do you want them back?' said Julie, lifting her right foot and grabbing the shoe by the heel. She felt she would be glad to be rid of the shoes now, comfortable as they were. She had a vague memory of fairytales where accepting gifts was a dangerous thing to do. (Probably not as dangerous as making an oath without knowing what it would mean or killing a seagull who was working as a royal spy. Still, no need to make a bad situation worse.)

'No,' said Molly Red. 'I give them to you freely and without obligation. I hope they suit your needs.'

'They're fine,' said Julie absently, looking at Aisling. Aisling looked a bit spooked. Julie had seen her in her normal sardonic above-it-all mood, and she had seen her scared out of her wits; this was not either of those, but something in between the two and a little closer to 'scared' than 'normal'. She wanted to ask what had happened to put that look on her face but not in front of Molly Red and the queen.

Her hands twitched and she realised she had been on the verge of reaching out, as if to grab at Aisling's hands and draw her nearer. *That would be – no, that would be bad*, she thought, in a muddled sort of way. She wasn't sure why, and she wasn't sure she wanted to examine the impulse at all – only, she was glad to see Aisling again, fiercely glad, and even gladder that

Aisling was safe and well; and that wasn't something she was ready to let anyone know, least of all Aisling herself.

Aisling side-stepped away from Molly Red, in Julie's general direction, and bowed slightly to the queen. 'I take it you are the Queen-that-will-be?'

The queen folded her arms across her chest, the deerhide somehow managing to stay draped around her shoulders. 'I cannot tell a lie,' she said. 'Now tell me, Molly Red: what is your plan, your purpose?'

'My plan is to make a plan,' said Molly Red. 'My purpose is to oust the mad queen before she can destroy the City, and the Realms Between with it.'

'Indeed,' said the queen, touching Julie's shoulder. 'Then you will be helping this girl here to fulfill her oath?'

Julie took a step back and away from the queen, getting out of reach of her hands and moving closer to Aisling at the same time. Aisling followed suit a moment later, so that they were standing side by side.

'Of course,' said Molly Red, not batting an eyelid. Julie wondered whether Aisling had told her about the oath or Molly Red just had a really good poker face.

'You shouldn't be here,' said Aisling quietly. 'There are only supposed to be two queens in the City at one time.'

The queen shot an acidic look in Aisling's direction. 'I understand the ways of death far better than you, child,' she said, then added, looking at Molly Red, who was frowning as if she'd just noticed something amiss, 'But this much is true: the queen on the throne cannot remain on the throne if the City of the Three Castles is to live.'

'Good, we're all on the same page, then,' said Julie. 'So what do we do? We have to get rid of her, but how?'

'We have to get to the Tower first,' said Molly Red, still frowning at the queen. 'And the best way to do that is with a prisoner.'

There was a pause. The glare the queen was directing at Molly Red began to feel like a palpable thing.

Molly Red shrugged. 'I volunteer, since no one else will. The queen on the throne would like to take me in.'

'Good,' said Aisling, 'that's settled. And when we get there, what comes next?'

'I have an idea,' said Julie. She gestured towards the queen in the deerhide. 'You're the Queen-that-will-be. The queen on the throne is the Queen-that-is. The queen in the ...' She swallowed and squeezed her eyes shut for the length of a heartbeat before going on. 'The queen in the cage is the Queen-that-was. If we kill the Queen-that-was, that'll trigger the cycle, right? The Queen-that-will-be will become the Queen-that-is, and the current Queen-that-is will become the new Queen-that-was.'

'So we'll have to get to the cage or get her out of it,' said Aisling. 'How are we going to do that?'

'I'll take care of that,' said Molly Red.

'Great!' said Julie. 'We go to the Tower with you in tow as a prisoner, then when we're there we … we …'

'Put the Queen-that-was out of her misery,' said Aisling.

'Right,' said Julie, nodding. 'And then we've fulfilled our oaths, and you can open the gates and we can go home.'

The queen glared at Molly Red. 'The gates? I said nothing about opening the gates! It is not my wish that the gates be opened!'

'Oh, *what*?' said Aisling. 'We just offered to put you in charge, and you're not even going to help us get home? What the hell kind of ungrateful –'

'Bite your tongue, child!' snapped the queen. 'I owe you no gratitude.'

Molly Red shot a warning glance at Aisling and said, 'Watch what you say. Only the ruler of the City can open or close the gates.'

'The Wormwood Gate's still open, though, isn't it?' said Julie. 'We could go home through that one right this minute and leave you here to stew.'

Molly Red nodded to the queen, who was silently fuming. 'They could, you know,' she said. 'Of course, they'd have to find it first.'

'You have an oath on your head – on both your

heads,' said the queen. 'You cannot simply leave.'

'Watch me!' said Julie, and she turned on her heel and made for the door. Aisling followed her, a beat behind. Before she could leave the cottage, the queen cried, 'Wait!'

Julie turned and spread out her hands. 'Well?'

The queen's face was dour. 'What is your desire?'

Julie glanced at Aisling. 'Well. Apart from wanting to go home, it's … this place, it's … The streets are empty. The City feels dead. It's creepy, and I don't like it. It doesn't feel like a real place.'

'In a way, it isn't,' said the queen.

'It is!' said Molly Red.

'Well, you can't both be right,' said Aisling, rolling her eyes. 'And I'm not from around here, so maybe I'm wrong, but I'm on Julie's side. This whole place is more like a theme park than a city.'

Julie glanced sharply at Aisling, startled to hear her echo a thought she'd had herself not so long ago. 'Yeah, that's right,' she said. 'It's all fuzzy round the edges.'

'Because the gates are closed. Take these two,' said Molly Red, jerking a thumb in the direction of the two girls.

Julie shrank back, which brought her closer to Aisling so that their arms were almost touching; it was comforting to be next to someone familiar, and she wished she could tuck her arm into Aisling's without feeling horribly self-conscious and awkward.

'They're more real than anything the City can produce,' Molly Red was saying, 'and they make everything they touch more real.'

'We do?' said Julie.

'That doesn't make any sense,' said Aisling.

'Nothing about this place makes sense,' said Julie.

'True,' said Aisling. 'You'd think I'd be used to it by now.'

'They are the first to come to the City for too long, Your Majesty. The Wormwood Gate moves; it doesn't always lead to or from the City. The other gates are closed, even the tiniest ones that never let in anything bigger than a mouse. The City is dying because of it. The people are not allowed out onto the streets – by the Queen's law? Well, truth be told, there are precious few people left to go out and break that law. The mortals are not crossing the boundary, and so the City is not being fed. Those who are still here are fading day by day. They'll fade, or they'll leave for the other realms, and when the last of them is gone you'll have no City to rule over. Only stones.'

'Brick upon grey brick,' Julie murmured, and Aisling gave her a startled look.

'You like Louis MacNeice?' she said.

'Just that one poem,' said Julie. 'I like poems about places.'

Aisling grinned lopsidedly. 'Why does that not surprise me?'

187

Julie scowled. 'Why do you have a picture of me on your phone?'

She was expecting Aisling to roll her eyes and say something sarcastic and condescending, and then they could have a fight and be back to normal; but instead Aisling blinked and blushed and opened and closed her mouth a few times and finally looked at the floor and muttered, 'No reason.'

Julie felt another shiver in her stomach, this time a nice one, of a kind that she understood all too well. *I know exactly what the reason is.*

She let herself bask in that thought for a few happy seconds before realising that it was about her as well as Aisling, and soon she'd have to decide what to do with this new thing she'd figured out. That turned the shivering feeling into a strange swooping and plunging, more like writhing snakes than butterflies.

Molly Red went on, 'The City will wither slowly with only the Wormwood Gate to connect it to the lands of mortals, but the City will only be the first of the Realms Between to suffer; it will not be the last, and it will not suffer the most.'

'You speak as if you expect me to care,' said the queen.

'Why don't you?' said Julie. 'Isn't this your domain? Your kingdom?'

'Wait,' said Aisling. 'What was that you said about the Wormwood Gate?'

'It moves of its own accord,' said Molly Red. 'It won't always be in the City.'

'Then we'd better get a move on,' said Aisling, 'before it moves away and we get trapped. We can hash this out later, right?'

'Yeah,' said Julie, stepping in between Molly Red and the queen. 'Enough standing around and talking. We have a plan, don't we? So let's do what needs to be done. The queen on the throne sent me to catch Molly Red; let her think that I caught her.'

The queen snorted. 'And what shall I do while you are engaged in this plan? The streets are not safe for me.'

'We can guard you,' said Aisling, moving forward to stand beside Julie once more.

'Yes, and I think the pigeons will help,' said Julie. 'They hate the queen's seagulls enough that they'd be delighted for an excuse to fight them.'

'Pigeons and street-urchins for an honour guard,' said the queen. 'How far one can fall. Very well. You may guard me. You, and the pigeons, and whatever other allies you can find. Molly Red, do you consent to this plan?'

'It's the only one we've got,' said Molly Red, shrugging. 'I don't think I can come up with a better one.'

'Let's go, then,' said Julie, marching to the door and through it, not looking back to see if the others were following her.

'The horse,' said Aisling, and Julie turned back to see Aisling plucking at Molly Red's elbow. Seeing them side-by-side was a little disorienting, because Molly Red always seemed to be taller than she was. Aisling wasn't all that tall herself (though the boots must have added at least three inches), but next to Molly Red she looked like an Amazon.

'It's this way,' she said, walking past Julie and down a narrow dirt lane that Julie hadn't noticed the last time she'd been there. Sure enough, when they emerged from the lane into a broad paved street, there was a horse-trough and a horse tied up to it. Aisling patted the horse's nose and checked its saddle and bridle in a knowledgeable-looking way. 'There, now,' she murmured. 'Feel better now you've had a rest and a drink, don't you?'

'I will ride,' said the queen, staring at the horse in a strange way. 'That way, if danger comes, I can escape the easier.'

'Wouldn't it be best if you walked?' said Aisling, still petting the horse and not looking at the queen or even turning to face her. 'There aren't any horses on the street thanks to the queen's curfew. Not many pedestrians either, but it'd be easier to hide if you were on foot. Besides, the crucial part of this plan is Julie and Molly Red getting to the Tower. You and I are spectators until they're finished.' At that, she looked up and gave the queen a bright, cheerful smile.

The queen frowned at Aisling, seeming to think this over. Julie wasn't sure whether she wanted her to acquiesce meekly, because Aisling was talking sense and she wanted to get to the Tower and get the job over with as soon as possible, or to demand the horse in a fit of pique, so that she and Aisling would have a chance to talk without the other two overhearing.

'Very well,' said the queen reluctantly. 'Mortal girl,' she said, addressing Julie, 'take the horse. Molly Red, walk behind with me. We have much to discuss, where the ears of these mortals cannot hear us.'

Julie approached the horse nervously. She'd ridden ponies before, when she was a kid – Shetland ponies, not much bigger than St Bernard dogs. This creature was as tall as she was at the shoulder, and it looked at her with shrewd eyes that could probably tell at a glance how little riding experience she'd had and how scared she was of falling off and breaking her neck.

'It's OK,' said Aisling in a low voice. 'I go riding all the time. It's easy. I'll show you how.'

'If you're such an expert jockey,' said Julie, 'why don't you ride?'

'I'm not the one the queen gave the job to, am I? As far as the queen knows, I'm a prisoner still. It has to be you, Julie.'

'I don't even – how am I supposed to get up?'

Aisling's eyes darted between Julie and the horse. 'Hmm, she's a bit of a monster for a titch like you.

Here.' She dropped to one knee and formed a step with her hands. 'Rest your left hand on the saddle – no, the pommel, I mean, the front bit – yeah, that's it. Now, I'll give you a boost. Grab hold of her neck when your right leg's all the way over, and I promise you, you won't fall.'

Julie rested her right foot in the cradle of Aisling's hands and hesitated, struck suddenly by the oddness of their position: as if it were she who was the queen and Aisling was an attendant lord. *Like Sir Walter Raleigh with the cloak*, she thought, *except that probably didn't happen. Makes a good story, though.*

'Left foot,' said Aisling. 'You want to swing your right foot over her flank, so I'll boost your left. OK?'

Julie glanced over at Molly Red, who was talking to the queen in a voice too low for her to hear. She was a little curious, but mostly she was relieved; whenever she tried something scary for the first time, she found it easier when no one was watching. Of course, Aisling was there, but Aisling was there to help her, and though that usually didn't make a difference, it did now.

She took a deep breath and put weight on her left foot, leaning a little on the horse's shoulder. There was a vertiginous moment when she seemed to be hanging in mid-air without any adequate support, but then Aisling lifted her hands, and that gave her the boost she needed to get her right leg over the horse's side.

She fell forward a little, her arms going around the horse's neck and her breath coming out in a soft 'oof' before she could right herself and sit straight.

Aisling stood up and started adjusting the stirrups. 'Are you all right?' she said softly. 'I don't just mean the horse, I mean everything. Did anything happen?'

'I'm fine,' said Julie. 'The queen – I mean, the queen on the throne, the Queen-that-is – she was convinced that you and I were assassins sent by the Lord of Shadows. Something about a treaty, or … Who *is* the Lord of Shadows, anyway?'

Aisling looked thoughtful. 'Molly Red told me he was married to the Queen of Crows –'

'The one who wants to invade the City?' Julie asked.

'Well, Molly Red said she doesn't, not really. And she's not married to the Lord of Shadows any more. She kind of hates him now, by the sound of it.'

'Bad divorce?' Julie giggled.

'Exactly. Put your left foot in the stirrup. Does that feel comfortable? Not too loose?' Julie nodded, and Aisling moved around to the horse's right side. 'Something's gone wrong with this place, that's for sure.'

'That's what everyone we've met says,' Julie said, 'and it's not like I don't agree, but … we don't have any way to tell if they're right. What was it like before? Does anyone even remember?'

'It must have been more solid,' said Aisling,

adjusting the stirrup strap. 'Don't you think? Less like it's about to dissolve into mist.'

'I suppose so,' said Julie. 'But that wasn't … Do you really think it makes sense to replace one queen with another?' She leaned closer to Aisling and lowered her voice. 'This one doesn't seem as evil as the one on the throne, but she's still pretty unpleasant. And anyway, it's a stupid system they have here. They should change it.'

'Yes, they should,' said Aisling. 'Or we should. We should help them.'

She handed Julie the reins and glanced past her. Julie followed her gaze; Molly Red and the queen weren't talking any more but were staring at the two of them, Molly Red with a calculating look on her face, the queen just looking annoyed.

'They're waiting for us,' said Julie.

'Let them wait,' said Aisling. 'Riding is dangerous if you don't know what you're doing. I have to make sure that everything's set up right and that you have some basic knowledge, or else I might as well toss you off a building.'

Julie felt a rush of warmth beginning in her stomach and spreading upwards. *She likes me*, she thought, trying the idea out, the way she might try out a new shade of lipstick or a pair of shoes: examining it from different angles, in different lights, imagining how it might go with the things she already had.

'You hold the reins like this, see?' said Aisling, her left hand covering Julie's and shaping it so that the thumb and little finger slipped under the rein and the other fingers curled around it. 'And the same on the other side. Not too tight, or she'll start to walk backwards.'

'And when we're moving, I pull on the reins to make her stop?'

Aisling adjusted Julie's grip, sliding her hands down the reins until there was a big loop of loose leather flopping down between them. 'Yup, and pull on the left to make her go left and on the right to make her go right.'

'Like steering a car.'

Aisling frowned. 'Well … yes, but no. I mean, yes, it's kind of similar, but a horse isn't a machine. She's alive, this one, and very lively. You have to treat her with respect. You also have to maintain your authority, or else she'll decide she's the boss, and then you'll be in trouble.' She smiled wryly. 'One time, I went to the stables to ride and the only pony available was this dumpy little curmudgeon of a grey who was so stubborn he made mules look weak-willed. As soon as I'd mounted him, he took off for the haybarn and wouldn't move, no matter what I did. He just stood there, calmly eating hay while I had hysterics on his back. Even when it started raining, he didn't move! I had to wait for one of the instructors to find me.'

Julie looked at the horse she was sitting on in dismay, feeling very small and very unauthoritative. 'Couldn't you just get off?'

Aisling shook her head. 'I was only eight. I'd never dismounted without an adult to help me down. I was too scared to try.' She patted the horse's neck. 'Don't worry, though. This lady's just had a real gallop. She'll be too tired to go wandering off on her own. Isn't that right, girl?'

The horse shook her head and snorted, as if in answer, and Aisling laughed.

She's pretty when she laughs, Julie thought, and her stomach did a somersault.

'Before the sun sets, if you please, mortal children?' said the queen in a drawling sort of voice.

Aisling rolled her eyes but stepped away from the horse and made a clicking noise that the horse seemed to understand; it turned around in a semi-circle so that it was facing away from the water trough, then stopped, awaiting a further command.

'Which way?' said Aisling.

Molly Red strode past them, the queen hurrying after.

'Follow me,' said Molly. 'I'll lead you to a place where we can see the Tower, and from there you can figure the route out yourself. You'll need to tie me up or sling me over the saddle or something. I won't be very convincing as a prisoner if I go to the Tower on my own two feet.'

Aisling looked up at Julie. 'Now, to make her walk, give her flanks a squeeze with your legs,' she said. 'Keep the reins pretty loose, or she'll get confused and think you want to stop or go to one side.'

Julie took a deep breath and squeezed with her legs. Like magic, the horse did exactly what Aisling had said she would do: she started to walk forward in a slow, steady, relaxed gait that felt very peculiar from where Julie was sitting. There was a slight bobbing motion, like a boat moored in the sea, and Julie could feel the horse's sides expanding slightly as she breathed and see the bones and tendons of her front legs working as she walked. The view from up on the horse's back was not high enough to be dizzying, but still high enough to be strange and disorienting. She couldn't help thinking of the first time she'd had a window seat on a plane, looking down on the airport and the houses and the fields as they grew smaller and smaller in her vision, feeling as if the world had turned itself inside-out. The height of a horse's back was enough, it seemed, to do something similar.

'You OK?' said Aisling, and Julie could only nod, not trusting her voice.

Molly Red and the queen turned a corner, and Julie managed to get the horse to turn in the right direction on the first try, which left her feeling elated and powerful.

'I'm getting pretty good at this riding thing,' she said, as casually as she could manage.

'Yeah, well, don't get cocky,' said Aisling. 'Hopefully you can just keep at a walk until we reach the Tower, and nothing will happen. But, listen, if something does happen – if we have to split up or run away – you need to know how to make her go faster.'

Julie's heart started to pound. 'Isn't that dangerous?'

Aisling shrugged. 'There are lots of dangerous things in this city. Riding fast might be less dangerous than the alternative.'

'OK. What do I do?'

'Click with your tongue, like I did earlier – don't do it now, you'll set her off – and kick her with your heels. Then, if she's not going fast enough, do it again. Keep the reins loose, and you'll probably want to lean forward and grab her neck or her mane, just to be sure you stay on.'

'I don't like the sound of that.'

'I don't like the sound of you with a knife in your chest.' Aisling took in a long breath and let it out slowly. 'Listen,' she said in a quiet voice, angling her face away from the other two, 'Molly Red's pretty ruthless. I saw her kill the man she got that horse from. She used my knife to do it with too.'

'Your knife? You have a knife?'

'Technically, it's a blade on a multitool, but that's not the point. She killed somebody, and he wasn't even trying to hurt us or capture us. He hadn't done anything to us. I mean, he was trying to help us! She said he was a spy, but … she doesn't always tell the truth. And even if she had good reasons, well … what if she had good reasons to do the same to us?'

Julie thought this over in silence. 'But people come back. Don't they? Isn't that why this isn't "mortal realms"? People come back after they've died. In a different form, but still …'

'I guess so, but this guy – he had mortal parents, she said, but she called him a Betweener, said he'd been in the Realms Between for long enough that he wouldn't die for real. But that doesn't apply to you and me. At least, I'm pretty sure it doesn't.'

'I thought you looked pretty spooked when you came in,' said Julie. 'Is that why?' Aisling gave her a startled look, and Julie looked away, feeling warmth rising in her cheeks. 'Anyway, who was the guy? And why did she kill him?'

'He called himself Morgan something. He worked for the Queen of Crows. Molly Red said he was a spy.'

'Did she say anything else about the Queen of Crows?'

'Oh, yes! She said –' Aisling frowned, and glanced back at Molly Red and the queen in the deerhide. ' – she said she used to work for her,' she went on slowly, 'and the Queen of Crows doesn't know her loyalties have changed. And that the Queen of Crows is … how did she put it? "Queen of the Lands of Death".'

'Spooky.'

'I know,' said Aisling. 'Julie … whose side are we on?'

It struck Julie first that Aisling had said 'we', taking for granted that of course they'd be on the same side, and only afterwards that she had no idea what answer to give.

'I don't know,' she said. 'Not for sure. I don't know if we're on anyone's side. We're against the Queen-that-is, I guess, and … I suppose that means we're for Molly Red and the Queen-that-will-be. For now, at least.'

'I'm not so sure about that,' said Aisling, and she looked as if she was going to go on, but before she could finish what she had to say, Molly Red and the queen abruptly stopped walking. Julie let the horse walk on for a few steps before she remembered what to do; she gave a sharp tug on the reins, and the horse stopped, shaking its head and chewing on its bit.

'Look,' said Molly Red, pointing. Julie followed her finger and could just make out the top of the Tower of Light beyond the buildings, which were getting newer and taller as they came closer to the centre of the City. 'I must be slung over the saddle with my hands tied, if either of you has a rope.'

'I don't have a rope,' said Aisling, 'but – hold on –' She pulled the belt of her coat free of its loops. 'Do you want to mount first? I don't fancy lifting you up onto her back. I'm not sure I could heft you that high.'

Molly Red nodded, raised the hood of her top, and

without further warning put her hands on the saddle behind Julie and vaulted up into a sitting position. The horse didn't like that and snorted and neighed and trotted back and forth a few steps before Julie could calm it down with pats to the neck and clicking noises like the ones Aisling had used before. Just when the horse had quieted, and Julie's heart had begun to slow down, Molly Red shifted in the saddle, and by the time Julie had turned around to look, Molly Red was lying on her side across the horse's back like a sack of grain, her hands flung down below her head.

Aisling approached her with a dubious look on her face, proffering the belt. 'How do you want me to tie this? Should I make it easy for you to get free, or would you rather have a really convincing knot?'

'Don't worry about that,' said Molly Red. 'There's not a creature in all the kingdoms of Fae and mortals that can tie a knot that can hold me.'

Aisling shot a long-suffering look at Julie and crouched down to bind Molly Red's wrists.

'There,' she said when she was finished, 'and if it's too tight or you can't undo it, don't blame me.'

'I will follow you at a distance,' said the queen, walking past them without looking at them. 'I will be watching, so do not change your minds. I have powers at my disposal beyond your capacity to imagine, and it would not go well for you if you were to cross me.'

'Yeah, yeah, great and terrible vengeance, whatever,'

Aisling muttered. 'Come on. Kick her again, Julie. You can probably see the Tower better than me from where you're sitting.'

'Good point.' Julie kicked the horse into a walk again, shifting in her seat as it started to move, the extra passenger making the saddle feel cramped and uncomfortable.

'Listen,' Julie said as a thought occurred to her, 'you shouldn't come with us. You were supposed to stay in prison as a … as a hostage, to make sure I'd behave. 'It wouldn't look good if you came along with me as if you'd been released.'

'Huh,' said Aisling, 'Now that you mention it, it's funny that nobody found me. There were patrols around, but none of them seemed to be looking for me, specifically.'

'I was protecting you,' said Molly Red's voice, sounding a little strained by her odd position. 'Not on purpose, mind you. You've heard that I can't be found unless I want to be? That extends to my companions.'

Julie twisted a little to look at her, then gave up when she found that, no matter what she did, she couldn't see the expression on Molly Red's face without slipping dangerously low to the left. She satisfied herself with asking, 'Then who counts as a companion? Does your woman in the deerhide count, even though she's off to the side?'

'Yes,' said Molly Red. 'She is travelling with me, even if at a distance. That's why the queen's seagulls haven't tried to peck her to ribbons already, though –' She cut herself off abruptly, and suddenly laughed. 'She wasn't happy to hear that.'

'I bet she wasn't,' said Julie, picturing the look on the queen's face when she realised she had to depend on Molly Red for protection. 'So … what do you think she'd be like, as a queen? Do you think she'd be a good ruler?'

'The important thing is getting rid of the one the City has now.' Molly Red's voice dropped low. 'That one there doesn't have to come next. Be better if she didn't, for more reasons than one.'

They were close to the Tower of Light now, and Julie could see a wide tree-lined avenue peppered with statues that led to the gated compound containing the Tower itself. Between getting there by being carried by seagulls and getting away by running like the clappers with both eyes out for guards, she hadn't yet had a chance to really look at the Tower, much less the approach to it, and the experience of seeing it now was a little dizzying, like the moment when an optical illusion would switch from one image to the other and back again, or like the times when she had seen a girl from a higher year in school and immediately known whose sister she was.

If they had been in the real Dublin there would have been a bridge over the river; there would have been people on the bridge selling T-shirts and cheap jewellery, and buses trundling past, and a smell of fermenting barley wafting down from St James's Gate. As it was, there was no river (but it had been there earlier – where had it gone?), no bridge, no jewellery stall, no scent of beer or horse dung or urine or car fumes; the buildings more than twenty feet away were misty and indistinct, and even the ground below her looked a little uncertain of itself, as if it might forget how to be ground if it were distracted.

And the avenue wasn't O'Connell Street; didn't even look like O'Connell Street, not really. There was a giant pillar with a statue on it just before the gates to the compound, for one thing, and no McDonald's or Burger King or Foot Locker or bank machines. The GPO was still there, a little scorched-looking, and the O'Connell Monument still dominated the southern end of the avenue and still had bullet-holes in random places, which raised a question Julie couldn't begin to answer: had the Easter Rising happened in the City of the Three Castles, just as it had happened in Dublin? Or had the effects of the Rising seeped through, somehow, leaving scorchmarks and bullet-holes in the City without the battles that caused them ever happening there?

But the resemblance ended there. Past the tall stone pillar was a stone wall interrupted by a high wrought-iron gate, and past the wall was a round tower the width of a house, made of a gleaming silvery metal and reaching high into the sky. Julie craned her neck to see the top; she could just about make out the cage containing the Queen-that-was, hanging below what looked like the current queen's chamber, complete with floor-to-ceiling windows.

It occurred to Julie that, high as the Tower was, and big as the windows were, the queen could probably see the entire City from there. No doubt she seldom left it.

'We should split up now, I guess,' said Aisling as they passed the O'Connell Monument. 'I can just hang around under one of those trees or something while you do the needful. Um, actually –' She reached into her pocket and produced something that looked like a Swiss Army knife, only its cover was metallic rather than red. 'This is my multitool,' she said, handing it to Julie, who had to fumble awkwardly to get it into her bag without letting go of the reins. 'It's got two knife blades, and a saw, and pliers and scissors and screwdrivers and – well, anyway. It's a handy thing to have.'

And it's already proven its worth as a murder weapon, Julie thought, but that was too dark a joke to make out loud.

'Thanks,' she said. She wanted to say more, but her throat had closed over. She could only hold Aisling's gaze as Aisling nodded gravely, said 'Good luck,' and turned to go.

But before Aisling was more than a few steps away, all three of them heard a sound that Julie, at least, had not heard since arriving in the City, so that it took longer than it should have done for her to realise what it was. By the time she knew it was a car approaching from around some corner or other, the horse had already grown alarmed and started to whinny and shake its bridle, and Aisling had whirled back around with a startled look on her face.

Julie yanked the reins – a little more forcefully than she had intended – and looked in the direction of the sound as the horse clattered to a halt. Sure enough, a car roared towards them from the direction of … not O'Connell Bridge, but where O'Connell Bridge would be if the Tower really stood on O'Connell Street. It was a taxi with its light switched off. It careered wildly across and down the road as if its driver was drunk and screeched to a halt halfway between the O'Connell Monument and the huge stone pillar – *Oh*, Julie thought, irrelevantly, *it's Nelson's Pillar; it didn't get blown up here* – and its driver stumbled out, muttering curses, and staggered and weaved towards the horse.

'Ah!' he said, and now that he was out of the car, Julie could see that it was Jo Maxi.

'What do you want?' she called out, trying to sound fearless and undaunted. There was a bit of a wobble in her voice that she hoped only she could hear.

'What do I want?' Jo Maxi shouted, waving his arms wildly. 'I want me fares back. I want to tear down the glass cages! I want to drown out the new chimes!

I want things back the way they were, when this was my city as much as anyone else's!' He laughed a bitter, hopeless little laugh. 'But since I can't have that, I want to cut off the head of Molly Red and sell it to the Queen of Crows.'

Julie felt a cold fist forming in her stomach and very carefully and slowly took a deep breath, and then another.

'Let's talk about this, shall we?' she said, watching and listening to herself from a distant place inside her head where she wasn't terrified. 'Let's not do anything rash.'

9

Taking her cue from Julie, Aisling started walking slowly towards Jo Maxi, holding her hands out wide in a non-threatening posture. He didn't look like he was carrying a weapon, but she didn't want to risk provoking him if he had one concealed under his jacket.

'Why do you think selling Molly Red's head will make things better?' Julie was saying, so calm and collected that Aisling wondered whether she had an autopilot that kicked in when things got scary. She had been calm when the seagulls had grabbed them and carried them away too, so calm and sure of herself that she'd been able to talk Aisling out of a panic attack. *Do you know?* Aisling thought. *Do you have any idea how brave you are?*

She felt a little ashamed of herself for being so easily scared, and then she felt even worse for thinking more about her own feelings than what was happening to the City, and she focused her gaze on Jo Maxi and watched and listened for an opening.

'It won't make things better,' he was saying in a hopeless sort of way, his gaze fixed on the ground and his face looking tired and droopy and sad. 'Nothing will. The City that I knew is dead. Dead and gone, and a new one springing up in its place. And that one's dying too. Dying before it was even properly born.'

'I'm trying to make things right,' said Julie. 'Please, let me get past you. I have something important to do, and I need to get to the Tower to do it.'

At that, Jo Maxi sprang to life as if he were Frankenstein's monster struck by lightning. 'The Tower?' He spat on the ground. 'The feckin' Tower? What makes you think I'll let anyone go to the Tower if I can stop them?'

'I'm trying to help!' said Julie, and there was a note of fear as well as frustration in her voice. 'I'm not a friend of the queen's. I'm with Molly Red.'

Jo Maxi's face distorted with rage. Aisling winced. That was the wrong thing to say. 'Molly feckin' Red! Sure, what did she ever bring us but lies and broken promises! Broken promises, can you believe that? And lies! Lies, she brought to the Realms Between, to the City, which was always a place where no lies could be told!'

He reached into his jacket and took out a wrench and a saw, brandishing them like twin weapons. Aisling stopped her slow movement towards him and lowered her hands a little. She looked at Molly Red, who lay across the horse's back, immobile, like a crash test dummy. *If she has any awesome destructive powers,* she thought, *now would be a good time to reveal them.* Molly Red's face was hard to read upside down, so Aisling couldn't be sure of her expression; what she could see was stern and stoical and not encouraging.

'Whatever issues you have with Molly Red,' said Julie, 'she's opposing the queen, and that makes her someone on the same side as me. For now, at least. The queen is sucking the life out of the City, and the only way to stop it is to bring her down.'

'Do you think the City can be saved? Is that it?' Jo Maxi threw back his head and laughed. There was a ragged edge to the laughter, as if he was a hair's breadth away from crying. 'What do yous know about that? Talk to the Ferryman and he'll tell you: everything dies. Everything! Even cities die, and this City's been dead for days. And it won't come back. The only hope for those of us left – few as we are – is to find a place somewhere else. And I mean to find Molly Red for the Queen of Crows and hand her over for a passport!'

Aisling glanced at Molly Red again. *Why isn't she saying anything?* she thought. *Why isn't she doing anything? Come to that, how was he able to find us?*

She looked from Molly Red to Jo Maxi and back again, and as Jo Maxi gestured shakily with the wrench and the saw and muttered to himself, wobbling on his feet, a startling thought struck her: *He can't see her. He doesn't know she's there!*

Carefully, with as little sudden movement as possible, she started walking backwards and to the left, and shifting her eyes and her head so that she could scan the sides of the street for the queen. When Julie looked in her direction, she seemed to notice what Aisling was doing and gave her a questioning look, but Aisling could only shake her head slowly and keep looking.

Molly Red can't hide us because we're standing right in front of him. But she can keep protecting the queen, as long as he doesn't see her. Does the queen know that?

'I'm still not sure why you want to sell Molly Red's head,' said Julie, 'or why you're standing in front of me like I can help you get it.'

'You said yourself you were with her, on her side!' Jo Maxi shouted. There was a sharp cry, and Aisling looked up to see seagulls whirring overhead. Her pulse started racing and she had to close her eyes for a second. *They can't see us. Are we protected? Are they too far away? Maybe they don't have good enough eyesight. Hawks have good eyes, but what about seagulls? I wish I knew.*

Jo Maxi took a staggering step towards Julie, and

another, and another. 'It can't be stopped, d'you hear? The City can't be saved.' The seagulls swooped lower and began to fly over his head, in a circle wide enough to include the horse and its riders. The horse snorted and shook its bridle, and Julie, startled, dropped the reins. When she picked them up again, Aisling could see she wasn't holding them right.

There was a flash of white off to the left, behind a pillar. Aisling let her eyes dart over in that direction to confirm that it was the queen's dress she'd seen, then looked back. Her heart started to throb painfully.

'I don't know why you're even talking to this guy,' she said loudly. 'If I were you, I'd just ride past him through the gates of the Tower.'

Another flash of white in her peripheral vision. Jo Maxi was looking straight at Aisling now, and she didn't dare look directly at the queen to see if she'd got the hint. 'What can you do, anyway?' she said to him. 'We don't know where Molly Red is. Go and look somewhere else.'

'Why do you want to give her head to the Queen of Crows?' Julie said more quietly.

Jo Maxi stopped walking and stood still, not even swaying. He still looked a little drunk, but not any more as if he couldn't control his body, only maudlin and emotionally volatile. Aisling started shuffling sideways in Julie's direction. He would be more dangerous like this.

'Because I have no place in the Kingdom of Crows,' he said. 'Unless I can give the queen something she can't get any other way. Do her a boon that nobody else can do for her. Then she'll give me a place, and when the City gets swallied up by the Kingdom, I won't get swallied up with it.'

'But why would she want Molly Red?'

'Not Molly Red. Molly Red's head, to put on a spike outside her palace, where she keeps the heads of traitors.'

He started to advance towards Julie, his eyes fixed upon her. Aisling took the opportunity to stare openly in the direction of where she'd last seen the queen. Sure enough, when she scanned up the left side of the street, she saw a white-clad figure creeping towards the gates of the Tower, dashing between trees and statues, trying to spend as little time as possible away from cover.

Aisling reached Julie and the horse before Jo Maxi did and tugged at Julie's hand, correcting her grip on the reins.

'When I say "go",' Aisling whispered, 'kick her and kick her again. Get her through the gates.'

Julie frowned. 'But the gates are –'

'I'll kill her with this,' said Jo Maxi, brandishing the wrench, 'and then I'll cut off her head with this,' waving the saw, 'and the Queen of Crows'll let me in then. Oh yes. Maybe give me Molly Red's old job too.

But first you have to tell me where she is, and don't you dare tell me you don't know!'

The seagulls started to cry. Aisling looked up at them, then forward, past Jo Maxi and towards the Tower. The gates were open.

This is it, she thought. *My turn to be brave.*

She walked forward three steps, enough to put her more than an arm's length from Jo Maxi – far enough away that he couldn't hit her with a wild swing of his wrench or saw, but close enough that she could jump him at a moment's notice. 'I don't think the Queen of the City would be too pleased if she found out about you,' she said loudly.

'I don't give a gnat's fart for the Queen of the City,' said Jo Maxi, and he spat at Aisling's feet, missing her boots by a bare inch. 'She's as much doomed as the rest of us, eejit that she is.'

Is that enough? Aisling thought. She glanced upwards. It was hard to tell, but she thought perhaps the seagulls' circling had slowed a little, as if they were preparing to swoop.

'Anyway,' she said, just as loudly as before, 'I don't know why you think I can help you. I'm not travelling with Molly Red.'

She repeated the last sentence in her mind a few times, just in case saying it wasn't enough. *I'm not travelling with Molly Red. I'm not travelling with Molly Red. I'm not travelling with Molly Red.*

There was a single loud cry, and then a chorus of shrieks, just as there had been when she and Julie had been on the roof.

Jo Maxi looked up, puzzled, his hands dropping to his sides, and Aisling lunged forward and tackled him to the ground. 'GO!' she yelled. 'Go, now!'

Through the shrieks and the sudden circle of beating wings around the two of them, she couldn't be sure of what she was seeing and hearing, but she thought she saw the horse springing into a trot, and then a canter, and she was almost sure she heard Julie's voice saying something, though she had no idea what it could be.

The seagulls whirled around them a few times. Then the pecking started. Aisling had thought her coat might protect her, and it did, a bit; but the seagulls got wise to this more quickly than she would have credited, and they pecked at her head and her neck and her legs, the only parts of her that weren't protected. It hurt, like being stabbed with a hundred tiny blunt knives, and Aisling thought perhaps she could give in, surrender, tell them they could take her in, slam her back in the cells, she didn't care, she'd confess to whatever they wanted her to confess to if they would only *stop the infernal pecking*; but no matter how still she lay, they wouldn't stop, and when she risked lifting her head a little, she saw that Jo Maxi was flailing uselessly at the gulls with his wrench and his saw.

'Stop that!' she shouted. 'You're making it worse!'

Jo Maxi snarled and shook his wrench at her. 'You arselicker! I'll show you worse!' He swung the wrench in her direction, and she ducked, but not quickly enough.

I rather think I brought that on myself, Aisling thought dazedly, and then there was nothing but darkness.

*

Julie yanked on the reins, and the horse reared.

'Whoa, there!' she cried, which was something she'd seen riders do in films.

It worked; the horse settled down, and when she pulled more gently on the left rein the horse turned in a semi-circle to face back towards the gates, which were now closed, a pair of horse-head guards stationed on either side.

Through the bars of the gates, she could see the flock of seagulls taking off into the sky and a prone figure on the ground – only one, and it was wearing a long black coat.

What happened to Jo Maxi? she thought, her heart pounding. She let go of the reins and slid off the horse's back, landing awkwardly on her left foot and hobbling as fast as she could towards the gates. 'Let me out!' she said to the guards, who said nothing and did not stir, as motionless as statues. Aisling's body was lying still.

With a cry, Julie launched herself at the gates,

grabbing onto the bars and pulling herself up as high as she could. She didn't get very far before the metal bars suddenly turned ice-cold under her fingers and she had to jump down. A heavy hand came down on her shoulder and a voice she had never heard before said, 'No running. You are in my power now, and she is in my domain.'

A cold dread gripped Julie. She gritted her teeth and turned around.

The hand belonged to a tall black-haired woman with skin as pale as chalk, dressed in a gown of black feathers, with a crow perched on her right shoulder. Julie had never seen her before, but there could be no doubt about who she was.

'Now,' said the Queen of Crows, her hand gripping Julie's shoulder momentarily so that Julie felt the prick of talons, 'to the Tower. You have an oath to fulfil.'

The queen removed her hand and turned around, and as she turned Julie thought she heard the rustling of dead leaves or grains of sand.

A kind of mist enveloped the Queen of Crows as she walked, weaving into the image of the woman in white with a deerhide round her shoulders and then quickly dissipating. Julie thought back over the things she and Aisling had asked the woman in the deerhide and the replies she had given, and realised that she had never said in so many words that she was the Queen-that-was; Julie had made an assumption, and the Queen of Crows had not corrected her. *I cannot tell a lie*, she had said, and that was most likely true.

'Can I leave you to take care of this?' the Queen of Crows said to Molly Red, who was still lying athwart the horse's back.

'Of course, Your Majesty,' said Molly Red.

'There's no "of course" about it,' said the Queen of Crows. 'That man with the weapon was right to say you brought lies and broken promises to this city. It is a skill of yours to lie or to twist the truth.'

'I thought you valued that skill, Your Majesty,' said Molly Red. 'I have put it to use in your service many times before.'

'And against me too?'

'Never!'

'Tell me, does he know something I do not, that crazed man? He said you were a traitor. A traitor to *me.*'

'Because I came to work for the queens of this city. He didn't know I came here on *your* orders.'

'Don't think I don't recognise this horse,' said the Queen of Crows. 'You could have enlisted the Count's aid, but you chose to take his horse and leave him to walk the paths back to the Kingdom of Crows. Why?'

'I prefer to work alone, Your Majesty. You know this.'

'And that is why I find it hard to trust your loyalty. You prefer to work where you cannot be watched. And so I must come traipsing after you, to watch you myself!'

'There was no need for that. I work only in your service, Your Majesty. I have been working steadfastly here to fulfill your commands.'

'But the queens still rule the City, and the treaty still holds. When the Lord of Shadows no longer has free passage through this City, I will count your loyalty as proven. Until then ...' The queen glanced at Julie. 'Watch your step. Both of you.'

With that, the crow on her shoulder took flight, and the Queen of Crows vanished.

The guards by the gates came back to life. 'How did you get over there?' one of them said. 'Wait, never mind. Um. HALT! Yes, that's it. Yes, um ...'

'Oh, let me handle this,' said the other one. 'You're rubbish at it. You, missy! What are you doing? What is your business at the Tower? Give us a good reason why we shouldn't arrest you!'

Julie glanced at Molly Red, whose expression was pretty blank. *No wonder the Queen of Crows doesn't trust her*, she thought. *I don't think I trust her myself.* There were things going on that Molly Red had never mentioned, plans and schemes and plots. The expression 'wheels within wheels' came to her mind, and for the first time, Julie thought she knew what it meant.

She was right, though, Julie thought. *I do have an oath to fulfil.*

She spared one last glance for the black-clad body

beyond the gates, squeezed her eyes shut for a second, two seconds, three seconds, then opened them again and gave the guards a hard stare.

'I have a prisoner for the queen,' she said, walking slowly over to where the horse stood. 'See?' she said, gesturing to Molly Red. 'The queen asked me to bring her news from Molly Red. I brought her Molly Red herself.'

'Oooh!' said the first guard. 'That'll make her happy!'

'Will you shut your fat trap?' said the second guard. 'All right,' he said to Julie. 'Take her up.'

Julie walked around to the horse's other side, wondering for an unsettling moment whether it was strange for the horse-head guards to see an ordinary, non-talking horse. She tugged at Molly Red's ankles, pulling her downwards over the horse's back until she slid down of her own accord, landing smoothly on her feet. 'Come on,' she said, grabbing her by her bound wrists and dragging her towards the Tower's front door.

The helmeted guards at the door saluted her and opened the door before she reached it. She marched through, Molly Red keeping pace at her side.

She had reached the end of a corridor and turned around three corners before she calmed down a bit and began to wonder exactly how large the Tower was on the inside and whether she ought perhaps to ask for directions. But just as she was about to say something to that effect to Molly Red, she turned a fourth corner and came upon a staircase – *the* staircase; the same staircase the horse-head guard had carried her up when he had brought her to see the queen.

Now that she was there with a prisoner of her own, she could see why the guard had had orders to carry her up. The stairs were so narrow that the two of them couldn't possibly ascend them side-by-side.

She pushed Molly Red forward. 'Go on,' she said in a clipped voice. 'You go first, I'll walk behind.'

Molly Red hesitated, turning her head to face Julie. 'She might come back, you know,' she said quietly.

'Who? The Queen of Crows? And by the way, were you ever going to tell either of us that that wasn't the queen of the city in the deerhide? Or was that another one of your super special secrets?'

Molly Red shook her head. 'The Queen of Crows won't return for a long time, if she ever does. No, I meant Aisling.'

For a split second, Julie wanted to punch her. 'Don't *say* things like that!' she whispered. 'Don't – you can't say things like that about somebody who's …'

She trailed off. She couldn't say the word.

'You know that life and death are not the same here as they are in mortal realms,' said Molly Red. 'That's why we call them mortal realms. There's a power that the Queen of Crows has in the lands where death is final.'

'You mean she doesn't have power *here*? Because I kind of got the impression she did, what with the freezing and the illusions and … stuff.'

'Oh, she has power, of a kind. But why do you think she needed to use an illusion at all? She can't walk openly through another ruler's territory because in their own lands they have the advantage. She has the advantage in her own kingdom and in the Land of the Dead – the land on the banks of the River – but in the realms of the Fae and the Realms Between, she is no more powerful than I.'

'But –' Julie frowned. Part of her wanted Molly Red to explain, preferably with a diagram and maybe a map, but there was only one thing that really mattered to her right that moment. 'So – Aisling is … She said Aisling was in her domain. Does that mean … is she back in mortal lands?'

Molly Red shook her head. 'Most likely she's at the banks of the River.'

'What river? The Liffey?'

'You know the way people here have names that tell you who they are, or make-names that tell you who they want you to think they are? The River doesn't have a name at all. It's just the River. It's older than names, and the magic of names doesn't touch it.'

'So … Aisling is … this river, it … it's like the Styx? The river that leads to the land of the dead?'

Molly Red shrugged. 'Sort of. I've crossed it eight

times and never known where it would lead if I let myself float downstream. Not sure anyone knows, even the Queen of Crows herself. But I'd bet seven of my nine forms that Aisling's at the River's bank right now, and knowing her, she's probably giving the Ferryman a run for his money.'

Julie stared at Molly Red's face. *It is a skill of yours to lie*, the Queen of Crows had said, and yet Julie didn't think Molly Red was lying now. 'So she might come back,' she said, trying to ignore the leaping of her heart. 'She might not be … gone … for good?'

'I know better than most that there are ways around the River. Ways to cross it without paying the Ferryman's fee. She's a clever girl, your friend. She can puzzle her way across it, or under it, or past it, and find her way back here or back to your own city.'

Julie stood still, staring at the walls and thinking. It was still a 'maybe', an 'if', a possibility rather than a fact. *I'll act as if she's … gone*, she thought, wincing away from the word even in her own head. *Because it would be … if I thought … if I hoped, and then …*

Tears sprang to her eyes and she took a deep, slow breath to push them back down. *I could at least have told her*, she thought, furious at herself. *I knew we were heading into danger and I never even –*

She grabbed Molly Red's arm and turned her around to face the staircase. 'Go on,' she said. 'Go up.'

*

Aisling woke up to the sound of water lapping against stone. The ground beneath her was cold and hard, and her head hurt. She groped on either side to make sure it was safe and carefully pulled herself upright without opening her eyes.

Paracetamol, she thought. She always had paracetamol in case of an emergency.

She felt through her pockets one by one, thinking as she did so that she really should get some sort of bag, like a doctor's bag, maybe, with labelled compartments, because all of her stuff was getting squashed and dusty, and it was impossible to find what she needed when she needed it. Her fingers finally closed on a small, slightly flattened rectangular box, and she pulled it out and opened it, only to find that what came out when she shook it was not a blister pack of pills but a pungent-smelling cigarette.

She opened her eyes. *That's not right*, she thought. *I gave the cloves to Molly Red, and she never gave them back.*

Her headache was fading anyway, so she abandoned the search for painkillers and examined the cigarette packet. It was the same packet she'd given to Molly Red: same brand, same packaging – even (she tipped out the cigarettes and counted them) the same number of cigarettes.

But she burned some of them down, she thought. *I don't know how many exactly, but at least two.*

She put the cigarettes back in the box and looked around. The light was dim and diffuse, as if it came from everywhere and nowhere in particular; she was in a place she didn't recognise, on the bank of a river that had once been deep and wide, to judge from the highwater marks on the opposite bank, but had now shrunk down to a tiny stream, no more than twenty feet across.

There was a ferry perched incongruously in the water, taking up so much of it that Aisling could have jumped from the far end of the ferry to the other bank. On the ferry stood a hooded and cloaked old man with a punting-pole and a sour expression. He was staring at Aisling in a distrustful way. Aisling decided straight away that she didn't like him, and she would put off talking to him as long as she could manage.

She got to her feet, stuffing the cigarettes into her pocket, and walked up the slope that led away from the River. The landscape was mostly pretty blank, with a soft greenness underfoot that wasn't grass or moss but something vegetable that felt like carpet to her feet and like reeds to her fingers. A little way on, the slope eased away and then got steeper, turning into a proper hill. In the side of the hill was a doorway with a stone lintel and threshold. Aisling peered in the doorway and saw a stone-lined corridor that looked human-made, not like a natural cavern, though the light petered away after about ten feet, and there was no way to be sure whether there was a natural cavern deeper in.

She hadn't brought her pencil torch with her, and Julie still had her phone, which made the prospect of an impromptu spelunking session very unattractive. She turned her back on the doorway and surveyed what she could see from its threshold: the land sloping down towards the River, the riverbed that was mostly dry, the ferry and the man standing on it. The opposite bank was wrapped in mist, and so was the top of the hill and whatever lay farther up or down the River.

Aisling steeled herself and walked down towards the ferry.

'From everything I've heard, I imagine you're the Ferryman,' she said when she reached it. The man nodded wordlessly, his expression still sour and distrustful. 'Well, maybe you can explain a few things. Where are we?'

'This is the River,' said the Ferryman with a voice like the pages of an old book rustling and crackling as they were turned by an ungentle hand.

'I can *see* that,' said Aisling. 'Obviously it's a river. Sorry, *the* River. I mean, this is a mostly featureless landscape surrounded by fog, and I'm guessing that if I walk into the mist, I'll either bonk into an invisible wall or come out again at a slightly different point along the River, right?'

'No one who has walked into the mist has ever returned,' said the Ferryman.

'Oh,' said Aisling. 'Well,' she said, rallying, 'anyway,

you're – is your name Charon?'

'I have been called Charon.'

'But it's not your name. Of course not. That would be too simple. You're the Ferryman, you've got the ferry, you bring people across the River that divides life from death –'

The weight of what she was saying caught up with her, and she had to pause and take a breath. *I died*, she thought. *I died, but here I am. Huh.* 'S-so anyway – I lost my thread. Give me a second. Yes, you – you decide, don't you? What form the creatures take when they cross over? That's what Molly Red said.'

The Ferryman nodded.

'And, uh, does that – does that apply to everyone who dies in the City?'

The Ferryman nodded again.

Tears prickled at the corners of Aisling's eyes. She bit her lip and sucked in her cheeks and clenched her teeth to keep them from flowing over. 'Including me?'

The Ferryman nodded. Aisling let out a gusty breath. She wasn't dead! Not really and truly rung-down-the-curtain-and-joined-the-Choir-Invisible dead. There was a chance. There would be more life for her.

There *could* be more life for her.

She didn't want to ask, but she'd been raised by lawyers, and she knew all too well what happened to people who signed contracts without reading the fine print.

She bit her lip and met the Ferryman's eyes. It gave her an unpleasant itching sensation in her mind that she did her best to ignore.

'What's the catch?' she said.

The Ferryman shrugged. 'No catch.'

'Oh, come on. Immortality for anyone who dies in the City, even if they're not from there? That's way too good a deal. And my mum always says that if something looks too good to be true, it probably is. What's the catch, Ferryman? How does it work, and what does it cost?'

The Ferryman sighed, a sound like wind rushing through a pile of dry leaves. 'The price of the crossing is two coins.'

'Any two coins?'

The Ferryman nodded.

'And what happens then?'

'I cannot tell you that.'

'"Cannot tell me" as in you swore a binding oath that you wouldn't, or "cannot tell me" as in you'd rather not?'

'I cannot tell you.'

Aisling scowled. 'You are positively the least forthcoming person I have met in the past forty-eight hours,' she said, 'and that's saying something. OK. You can't tell me what happens after you take me across the River, correct?'

The Ferryman nodded.

'Well, what if I found a way to cross without taking the ferry? What would happen then?'

The Ferryman's mouth twitched and his eyes grew distant. It had the effect of shifting his expression entirely from 'sour and distrustful' to 'childishly afraid', which was almost enough to melt away Aisling's dislike of him.

'I am the Ferryman,' he said after a long pause. 'I carry the dead to that which lies after death. I have done this for as long as I have been. I have done this for as long as the River has been.'

It had the air of a recitation from memory, chanted now more as a way of reassuring himself than because it was relevant or true, and Aisling would have ignored it if the River hadn't suddenly surged up around the ferry and slopped over onto his feet, wetting the hem of his cloak. The Ferryman blinked, looking even more afraid than before, but he did not look down.

Aisling did, and in the swirling of the River she saw what looked like faces, their eyes and mouths wide open, terrified – screaming? They made no sound, and every eddy of the water would break up one face and form another, no two of the faces looking alike.

'What's going on?' she said. 'What's up with the River?'

'The River has always been, since there have been living things on the earth,' chanted the Ferryman, still not looking down at the water that was up around his ankles now. 'The River is the threshold, and I am the one who carries those who must cross. The River is –'

'The River is full of screaming faces!' Aisling said, interrupting him. 'Is that normal?'

'The dead!' said the Ferryman in a hoarse whisper. 'It is the dead!'

'But – don't you carry the dead across?'

'I carry only those who have the fare,' said the Ferryman. 'For those with no fare –'

'They try to swim, but they never make it across, do they?' said Aisling, taking a step back from the water as she spoke. 'They get trapped in the water.'

The Ferryman said nothing in reply, but he closed his eyes and swallowed hard. Aisling shook her head in disbelief.

'You send them into the River if they don't have two coins? So the poorest people end up as watery ghosts?'

'It is their choice!' the Ferryman said through gritted teeth. 'I have the power to deny a crossing. I have no power to force a soul into the River.'

'And if they can't take the ferry, and they don't go into the River, what other choice do they have?'

'I cannot say,' said the Ferryman, his eyes still squeezed tight shut.

'Oh, bullshit!' said Aisling, longing for a stick to hit him with, since she was too far away to slap him. 'Look at me! What happens to them? Where do they go?'

The Ferryman opened his eyes and stared at her, once again giving her that uncomfortable itching sensation. 'Grant me a boon and I will give you what you want,' he said.

'That's more like it,' said Aisling. 'Not that I want to do you a favour, but … all right. What do you want?'

'All that I ask in exchange for the knowledge you seek is this: release the River.'

'Release the River?'

The Ferryman nodded.

'I can't agree to that! I don't even know what it means. How am I supposed to release a river? How does a river get un-released in the first place?'

'*Look!*' the Ferryman hissed. 'Look at the River! Look where it once was and where it now is! It dwindles to nothing!'

'And why is that? Is that because there aren't any more souls getting trapped in it?'

The Ferryman shook his head with a wince, as if Aisling was so wrong it pained him. 'If never another soul entered the River from this day on, it would still be deeper and wider than any river that flows through mortal lands.'

'Then why –'

'The Queen of Crows!' the Ferryman whispered. 'She would block off every path the Lord of Shadows might travel to do his work. She has quenched the lights in the labyrinth, so that there are no shadows for him to travel through, and dammed up the River upstream of the crossing. Even I, her most loyal servant –' He glanced down at the River, where its waters lapped around the edge of the ferry, and swallowed audibly. 'I have ever been loyal to the Queen of Crows. She does not repay that loyalty.'

He screwed his mouth up tight at that, as if he had said too much. Aisling pondered for a moment, finally saying, 'OK, so ... how do I un-dam the River, then? I don't like my chances if I go up against this Queen of Crows.'

'I cannot tell you.'

'Then I can't promise you anything.'

'There are those who know. Likely, the queens of the City know. Likely, Molly Red knows,' said the Ferryman.

'Molly Red doesn't tell what she knows unless she thinks it'll do her some good,' retorted Aisling. 'I can ask her, but that doesn't mean anything will come of it.'

The Ferryman fixed her with a glare that made her stomach churn.

'There are ways to compel even her, the wild one,' he said. 'There are ways to force her hand and ways to persuade her. You can use those ways. If you do not swear to release the River, I will tell you no more.'

'But even if she tells me how to free the River from the dam, how am I supposed to actually do it? Am I supposed to tell you I will, without even knowing what it is?'

'Do you agree or not?'

'I didn't say I didn't agree. I'm thinking.' Aisling frowned and turned her back on the Ferryman, wanting to think without that unnerving glare to distract her. A moment later, she turned back around. 'All right,' she said, 'here's the deal. You let me know what I want to know, and I'll swear to *ask* Molly Red how to release the River, and if it's something I feel I can do, I'll do it. But no guarantees! And you have to pony up the information before I make the promise. Agreed?'

The Ferryman's lips twitched, and his expression regained some of its previous sourness. 'Agreed,' he said.

'Well?' said Aisling. 'I'm waiting. What's the third choice? Or, I should say, the fourth. People who have the fare cross over on your ferry. People who walk into the mists don't come back. People who swim the River end up as ghosts. What else can you do if you don't have the fare for the crossing?'

'I cannot *say* what happens to the dead who do not cross the River,' said the Ferryman, and for a moment Aisling thought he was messing with her, but the emphasis on 'say' was strong enough to make her look for some other clue. He wasn't looking straight at her any more but staring over her shoulder. She followed his gaze, all the way to the stone doorway in the side of the hill.

'Oh,' she said. 'You have got to be kidding me.'

'I never kid,' said the Ferryman.

'I believe you,' said Aisling grimly. 'All right. I swear that I'll ask Molly Red how to release the River, and if it seems like something I can do, I'll do it. Now, do you have a torch, by any chance?'

The Ferryman shook his head.

'No, of course not,' Aisling muttered. 'Oh, well.'

She set off towards the hill and the dark stone doorway.

10

Julie's mind was blank as she ascended the stairs. She could hear Aisling's voice in her head saying *No, you can't touch it; it's all fun and games until somebody loses an eye*, which was something she'd overheard her saying in class once. At the time she hadn't cared enough to turn around, but now she thought Aisling must have been showing off her multitool.

At the top of the stairs, she took the multitool out of her bag and unfolded the largest of its blades. She held it behind her back as she and Molly Red approached the door.

At her knock, there was the same series of clattering, clicking noises she had heard the last time, and the same guard as before opened the door and peered suspiciously at her. 'I have a prisoner for the queen,' she said. 'None other than Molly Red herself.'

'The notorious rebel, eh?' he said. He smirked and flung the door open.

As Julie escorted Molly Red towards the second set of doors, she thought about the things she'd seen and heard while she was in the City. The guards opened the doors for them and she pushed Molly Red through, and passed through herself. The queen's chair was turned so that the back was facing the doors.

'Your Majesty,' she said, 'I've brought you a prisoner.'

The queen spun round in her chair and grinned, her one eye fixing on Molly Red. 'Marvellous,' she breathed. 'I understand, now, why the Lord of Shadows uses mortals to do his work. You go the extra mile!'

The queen's obvious glee made Julie feel dirty. 'Yeah, well,' she muttered, glancing past the queen at the cage that was hanging from the Tower's top floor. She could barely see it from here, just a suggestion of metal bars swinging in the breeze.

The queen rose from her chair and strode slowly over to Molly Red. 'I wonder what punishment I should devise for you,' she murmured to her prisoner, rubbing her hands together. 'Cut your tongue out, perhaps, so that you can tell no more lies with it? Or would that be too crude? Perhaps I should cover it with a fiery pepper that never loses its strength, so that your mouth will burn every time you try to speak?'

'Oh, shut up!' said Julie.

Both the queen and Molly Red turned to look at her, the queen shocked, Molly Red, apparently, amused.

'You got everything wrong, you know,' said Julie. 'Well, not everything, I guess, but enough. You think you're saving the City from invaders, but you're killing it.'

'Hold your tongue, child,' said the queen, 'or I'll do the same to you as I do to her!'

Julie rolled her eyes. 'That's the problem, right there. You won't listen to anyone who challenges you! You wouldn't listen to me when I told you the truth because you were convinced I was lying, so then I *did* lie, and I don't know why you believed me then, because I was making it up as I went along. You're cynical and gullible at the same time. I don't know how you manage it, but it's messed everything up.'

'I told you to hold your tongue,' said the queen, her eyes narrowing.

'Right,' said Julie, 'because this is your territory, isn't it? And that's where you're most powerful? But I'm not so sure of that. Do you think you can change the way things work just by wanting them to be different? You never killed the Queen-that-was. Doesn't that make you the Queen-that-will-be, not the Queen-that-is?'

The queen's eyes gaped and her jaw fell.

'You know, that never occurred to me,' said Molly Red thoughtfully. 'But the mortal girl has got a point. You may have crippled your older sister so that she couldn't rule, but you're not actually queen yourself. Maybe that's why the City is in such a bad way.'

'It's not true!' the queen growled. 'It is not true! I am queen! I, and I alone!'

'I suppose if you say that often enough, it'll become true,' said Julie. There was a light, fizzing feeling in her stomach, and her head felt light too, as if she were very slightly drunk. 'But that doesn't mean it's true now. So tell me: why *should* I hold my tongue? Why should I be afraid of you?'

'I'll show you why!' the queen snarled, and she strode over to one wall of the chamber where there was a giant switch, the kind used for generators or to turn on a town's Christmas lights. 'Hand me that knife you're pretending not to carry.'

Julie hesitated, looking at Molly Red, who shrugged, smiling lopsidedly. The fizzing feeling came back, and though she couldn't think of a single reason to trust either of them, she felt very strongly that handing the multitool over was the right thing to do.

'All right,' she said, and held it out, handle first.

The queen took it, then threw the switch. The lights flickered and there was a humming noise and a muffled clanking, and the floor-to-ceiling window that surrounded the room started to retract and rise, as if it were being pulled up on invisible ropes, and on the outside of the Tower something started coming up and rising over the floor of the chamber.

It was the cage, and inside it the defeated Queen-that-was.

Julie felt a certain tightness on her skull fade away, and the lightness in her head and stomach vanished too. As the defeated queen rose to stand on shaky feet, she thought *The oath. I've fulfilled it. I swore I'd find a way to kill her, and I found one.*

Two down, one to go.

'I should have done this to begin with,' said the reigning queen, sniffing disdainfully. 'I should not have let you live. I will find another way to stop the cycle, be sure of that.'

'You will not,' said the ragged queen, her voice thin and croaky. 'The City will die from your foolishness before you do.'

'Silence!' The reigning queen strode towards the cage and flung its door open. 'Come!' she said, beckoning. 'Come to your execution.'

The ragged queen glanced at Julie, and though she didn't smile or move her lips, Julie thought she looked grateful. Julie nodded, and the ragged queen walked towards her sister – raggedness and all, emaciation and all, it was astonishing how similar they looked, down to the missing eye – and stood still at the threshold of the cage.

The queen raised her right hand and thrust the knife between her sister-self's ribs. The frail, ragged queen was still for a moment, then she crumpled, like a marionette whose strings had been cut; then she vanished into nothingness.

*

The light ran out ten paces into the stone-lined corridor, and Aisling stopped after the next step brought her into darkness, her heart trembling and her hands shaky. She knew her eyes would get used to it, as long as there was any light at all, and that since she had already died (a thought her brain seemed to skip over slightly every time it came up), there was nothing to be afraid of; and yet she *was* afraid, and no amount of rational thought would help. She tried to find that cool, logical self she had been when Molly Red had leapt onto the horse's back and spurred her into a gallop, but every attempt left her grasping at nothing and turning round and round in circles.

Aisling took a step forward, not knowing how, barely even knowing that she'd done it, as if her feet were moving of their own accord. Her hands too rose up to touch the walls at either side, feeling along the stones and wandering into the cracks between them.

Another step. Another. The darkness was no less thick, now; thicker, if anything, and her eyes were not adapting to it at all. Despite that, she could feel her brain thawing a little, the paralysis that had taken over beginning to recede.

If I keep my hand on the stone. If I take small steps.

More steps, now, still slow and small, but coming one after the other, without hesitations in between. Then the stone beneath her left hand fell away, and her heart dropped down as if it had fallen a hundred feet below her chest.

It's just a turning. A corner. It's not –

She stepped back, shuffled sideways so that she was right up against the left-hand wall, and crept forward with even smaller steps than before, so that the turning didn't take her by surprise, and so that she stuck to the left-hand wall when it came.

Keep your left hand on the left-hand wall. If you reach a dead end, keep your left hand on the wall and keep going, into the dead end and around again. That's the way to get out of a maze.

She'd read that years ago, and she'd never had a chance to test it, but her brain clung to it now just as her hand was clinging to the wall.

Logic. Logic and reason. I'm dead. I'm dead. I died. I – mind you, that was a pretty good death. I didn't think I had it in me. I hope Julie's all right.

She was calming down a little now. She had never thought of herself as being afraid of the dark, but then she had never been in a darkness as thick and impenetrable as this one. Deep in a cave in a hill shrouded in fog, in a land that probably never saw sunlight –

The Lands of the Dead. That's where it is. I woke up in the Lands of the Dead. So there is an afterlife after all.

She could feel the ground beneath her feet sloping downwards. The labyrinth twisted and turned more often than she could keep track of, and she had lost all sense of time long before entering it, so she had no idea how long it had been or how far she might have come when she took a step – a small, modest step, just like all the steps she had taken into the darkness – and had to jerk back suddenly to keep from falling into the nothing that opened up underneath her feet. She did fall, but backwards, onto the floor behind her, her coat cushioning her fall and her right hand instinctively scrabbling for purchase on the air.

She let her heart slow down a little before cautiously pushing herself to sit upright. She slid her hand forward and sideways across the stones beneath her, her heart sinking as she realised that there was a pit in the floor in front of her that spanned the width of the corridor.

Her first thought was that it might not be so deep as to be dangerous. Her second thought was that that wasn't something to take chances on, even if she was dead; to spend eternity with a broken leg would not be fun. She felt through her pockets for something heavy enough to make a sound when it hit stone, and settled on a pencil; when she dropped it down into the pit, she held her breath and counted.

One-one-thousand. Two-one-thousand. Three-one-thousand. Four-one-thousand. Five-one-thousand –

There: a muted clattering. Well. It wasn't a bottomless pit, but it was still deep enough to be dangerous.

Aisling sighed. She suddenly felt weary to the marrow of her bones. She couldn't give up. She wasn't going to give up. But there was nothing she could do. She wanted to weep from sheer frustration; she wanted to throw something, but all the things she had to throw were things she might need. She wanted to scream, *I'm here, I'm not dead, not really dead!*

Then the words of Abayomiolorunkoje came to her: *If I can help you, in any way that is in my power, I will come if you call for me. That is a promise!*

'Do I have to call you by name?' she said out loud. 'Because, firstly, I'm pretty sure that wasn't your real name you told me, and secondly, I'm very sure that I can't pronounce it. Which is why you chose it, isn't it? So that people would remember your explanation for it, not the name itself? That people tried to humiliate you, but God would not let them.'

'You are clever,' said a voice out of nowhere. There was a ticklish feeling on the back of her left hand that felt like an insect walking over it. 'And you are right. Abayomiolorunkoje is not my true name, and you do not need to call it to have my help. But let me be sure of one thing, little friend: do you need my help now?

243

I owe you one favour and one favour only. Call for me again and I will not come, unless it pleases me.'

The voice was not the warm, genial Nigerian-accented voice Aisling remembered. This voice was a little higher, a little sharper, and the accent was subtly different in a way she couldn't have named.

'I don't think I'll ever need your help more than I do now,' said Aisling fervently. 'I'm – I have to get out of this labyrinth, and this pit is in my way.'

'Well, then,' said the voice, 'I can help you with that. Or I can get you help, which is almost the same thing.'

The ticklish feeling on the back of her hand went away, and from a distance she heard a rushing, swirling sound, like water, or leaves, or beating wings. The sound grew louder and louder until she knew it to be wings for certain, and there were gull cries along the wingbeats, sounding eerie and loud in the enclosed space of the tunnel.

'This is the last time, spider,' said a croaky voice. 'You've kept us in these tunnels for far too long already. Now you've summoned us a third time, and when we've done what you ask, we'll never dance to your tune again, be sure of that!'

Spider? Aisling thought with a jolt, puzzle pieces clicking together in her mind. *No wonder his eyes looked weird. 'A fine place to sit and spin a web,' indeed!*

'Of course,' said the spider, 'or at least, unless I catch you again the way I caught you before.'

'That won't happen!' said the gull. 'We're wise to your ways now. We won't be fooled again!'

'Be that as it may,' said the spider, 'you have one favour still to do for me.'

'Yes, yes. What is it?'

'Take this girl to the other end of the labyrinth. Gently.'

'Can you all see in the dark or what?' said Aisling, who was conscious of a change in the atmosphere since the seagulls had arrived, a constant low-volume shuffling and scraping and a kind of pressure against the air that suggested she shouldn't make any sudden movements lest she accidentally punch one of them in the wing, but still she couldn't actually *see* anything.

'Of course,' said the spider. 'Can't you?'

'Ask a stupid question,' Aisling muttered. She rose carefully to her feet. 'All right,' she said. 'Take me to the other side. I'm ready.'

Her stomach lurched as the gulls massed around her and gripped parts of her coat and boots in their beaks. It was too like the first time this had happened to be comfortable, yet once they took off it was nothing like it at all. They flew slowly and carefully, not bumping her or scraping her with their wings or even varying the height they were flying at much. It was a little like riding stomach-down on a slightly wobbly conveyor belt, which was unnerving in itself; without having contact with the ground or the walls, she had no sense whatsoever of where she was or where she was going. She could have been floating suspended in a blank void and never have known the difference.

When the light came, she didn't believe it at first, assuming that the glimmer she saw was her eyes playing tricks on her. The seagulls had a grip on both ends of her coatsleeves, so she couldn't lift her hands to her eyes to rub them, but she blinked and squeezed them shut; and when she opened them again and found it had made no difference, and the light began to grow brighter, she allowed herself some cautious hope. It was probably not the exit, but it would be wonderful even if it was a lantern or a torch or a cluster of phosphorescent mushrooms.

She was expecting that eventually the light would grow brighter until she couldn't look at it any more, and then she would blink and be back in her body and back in the City; but in fact, as she and the gulls grew closer to the light it grew more distinct but not brighter. It was sunlight, she was sure of it, which irritated her, though she couldn't pinpoint why. There were hints of green in the distance, and no sign of buildings, and when the tunnel ended abruptly, leading out to a brightly green hill whose slopes were shrouded in mist, she almost swore out loud. The tunnels hadn't brought her back to the beginning, had they?

The seagulls set her down, more gently than the last time. She rubbed her arms and shook her legs out a bit. 'Thanks,' she said, and she looked around.

Down the hill she could see a narrow river, though whether it was *the* River, she couldn't tell. Uphill, there was a woman standing a little way away, with her back to Aisling, facing into the bank of mist.

'Hello there!' Aisling called out. 'Sorry to disturb you, but would you happen to know ...'

She trailed off, realising that she wasn't sure what question she wanted to ask. *Would you happen to know the procedure when a mortal dies in the Realms Between?* Or *Would you happen to know if I've been hallucinating this entire episode and I'm in a coma in a hospital bed somewhere?* Or maybe even *Would you happen to know what I should do next? Because, honestly, I have no idea, and at this point I'm sick of improvising. I'd kind of like somebody to tell me what to do.*

The woman turned around. She had one eye, the missing one being covered by an eyepatch, and she looked identical to the queen.

'Greetings,' she said. 'How did you come to be here?'

Aisling opened her mouth, closed it, frowned, and said cautiously, 'Forgive me, but that's kind of a long story, and I'd rather not get into it right now. What about you? Why are you here?'

'I am waiting for the mist to clear,' said the woman. 'It is solid now, to keep me from passing through to the City of the Three Castles. When it clears, that will mean that one of my sister-queens is dead, and I can go back safely and await my turn on the throne.'

Aisling closed her eyes and rested the heels of her hands over them for a second. 'So …' she said, lowering her hands, 'who might you be?'

The woman straightened her back, drawing herself up to her full height. 'I am the Queen of the City of the Three Castles. Not the Queen-that-is. The Queen-that-will-be. I was called too soon from the shores of the River – these very shores, indeed. I was called back to the City before the Queen-that-is had died, and yet the third of us held the throne. I know not how or why such a thing might be, and yet it was. And it was a great wrong, and greater still that I should be in the City with my two sisters still alive. Fortunately, there was one who knew this and took me back to the River's shore, though the route she took was a strange one, passing through the lands of mortals, and I had need to borrow the Ferryman's fee, for I had not a single coin, nothing to carry but the clothes on my back. And now I wait.'

'Right,' said Aisling, her mind reeling. The other one – the one they met in the City – she must have been an imposter. For a city where nobody could lie, there were certainly a lot of people pretending to be things they weren't.

The Queen-that-will-be glanced at the seagulls and frowned.

'These noble birds – are they your companions?' she asked.

'Oh,' said Aisling, 'um, sort of. They helped me through the labyrinth.'

One of the seagulls pushed itself past the others and bent its head before the Queen-that-will-be in a gesture not entirely unlike a bow.

'Our brothers and sisters in the City are servants of the Queen-that-is,' it said, 'and we'll be happy to serve you likewise, once the mist clears.'

'Wait a second,' said Aisling, 'do you mean none of us can get back until she does?'

'There are paths along the shore that lead to other lands in the Realms Between,' said the Queen-that-will-be. 'You can walk them, if your only desire is to leave the shores of the River. Whether any of the paths lead to the City of the Three Castles, I cannot say. This mist blocks the only path I know for sure to lead there, and it blocks the path so that there can never be three queens in the City at one time. And so I wait.'

Aisling looked down the hill and to either side. She couldn't see anything that looked like a path, only the kind of pseudo-trails she'd seen in parks and woods that never really led anywhere, just got you deep enough into the terrain to get thoroughly lost. 'I won't take the chance,' she said, sitting down. 'I'll wait with you. Unless,' she added, a thought occurring to her, 'you know about the dam on the River? The Ferryman thought you might.'

'A dam on the River? That would explain why it had shrunk to such a tiny stream. But, no, I know nothing of it.' She looked thoughtful. 'When I return to the City, perhaps – yes, when I return, I will know. I will sense it.'

'Good,' said Aisling. 'Good.' She looked at the seagulls, which were milling around aimlessly, pecking at the ground. 'While we're waiting, maybe you guys can tell me something: why *do* you serve the queen? Seagulls always struck me as independent sorts of birds. Not like, I don't know, falcons or parrots. They always seem to be at some human's beck and call, but not seagulls. They do as they like. Why don't you?'

The lead seagull shifted its head to one side to focus one beady eye on Aisling. 'We're practical birds,' it said. 'We'll eat anything we can. We're not above a spot of larceny if it keeps the littl'uns fed. But when the gates were closed, all of a sudden there was nothing to larcenate. No people passing through with their chips in their hands, no black bags full of precious dinners. And the pigeons were at us day and night, foraging where we used to forage. Sure, what were we to do? The queen promised us food, and we gave her our word and bond that we'd do as she said. You're right, it's not the way we'd rather do things, but a bird's got to eat.'

Aisling nodded. 'It's a classic story,' she said. 'Scarcity of resources triggers conflict among competitors who need access to those resources. Happens all the time.'

The seagull's head bobbed in what might have been meant for a nod. 'And since we started working for the queen, the pigeons have been worse than ever. Not bad enough they take the food from our beaks, they have to make it an outright war! As if we haven't enough to be worrying about! You ask me, they're just looking for an excuse to scrap and steal. Cunning little thieves, the flock of them!'

Aisling resisted the urge to point out that the seagull had admitted moments ago that seagulls were happy to steal if they had to and wondered to herself whether the real problem between the pigeons and the seagulls was that they had too much in common.

'I see,' she said.

'The mist is clearing,' said the Queen-that-will-be. 'Come! If you would come, come! Now, before my sister crosses the River and the mist thickens once more!'

The mist did look less thick than before. Aisling jumped to her feet and followed her. As they stepped through the mist, the seagulls fluttering past them, she felt a tingling, like a weak electrical shock, and for a second everything went white.

*

'There's no need of a cage, since there's no prisoner for it to hold,' said the queen, folding the blade away and tossing the multitool aside. Julie scrambled to grab it and unfolded the blade. She meant to wipe away the blood, but there was none. *Maybe fairies don't bleed*, she thought.

The queen raised a hand, and the cage disappeared, and the glass wall of the tower room lowered itself back into place. Julie looked at Molly Red and shrugged, trying to signal *What next?*

Molly Red smiled a secretive smile and winked and mouthed something that looked like *Patience*. Julie rolled her eyes. She wasn't sure she had any patience in her any more.

The queen turned on her heel to face the two of them. 'Well!' she said, dusting her hands off against each other, 'now that that's been taken care of, what shall I do with you two? A traitor and a spy?'

'I'm not a traitor,' said Molly Red. 'At least, not to you. I never swore an oath to you, I never claimed to be loyal to you. If I've been working against you, that doesn't make me a traitor.'

'And I'm not a spy,' said Julie. 'I know I told you I was working for the Lord of Shadows, but that was only because you wouldn't believe me when I said I wasn't. I've never even met the man.'

'Be that as it may,' said the queen with an airy, dismissive gesture, 'I must still punish you. Both of you.' She glanced out through the glass wall, at the place where the cage had been. 'Perhaps I was too hasty in destroying that cage. Perhaps I should make two new ones and hang you up in them, let the seagulls feed on you, hm?'

'That's just silly,' said Julie. 'Seagulls aren't raptors. They'll eat all sorts of things, but they won't try to eat a living human.'

'If I command them to, they will,' said the queen. 'After all, I am the one true ruler of the City of the Three Castles, the Queen-that-is. How should they dare to disobey me?'

The stones of the Tower seemed to ripple as she spoke. Julie's stomach twisted.

'I don't know,' said Molly Red. 'You'd be surprised how daring people can be when they get really annoyed.'

As if those words had been a summoning spell, the door burst open and, amid a flurry of white wings, Aisling and a woman who looked like a younger version of the queen strode in, the woman looking fierce and angry and Aisling looking flushed and winded. Julie rushed over to Aisling and grabbed hold of her arms, then squeezed her in a tight embrace.

'You're alive!' Julie said to Aisling. 'I don't believe it. I don't believe it!'

'Steady on,' said Aisling, but she hugged Julie back, and her arms around Julie's waist were warm and solid.

Julie pulled back a little, gripping Aisling's chin between her thumb and finger and staring into her eyes. 'It *is* you, right? You're not – you haven't been –'

'My friend Philippa and I had a plan for if something like this happened,' said Aisling. 'We each came up with a set of passwords in case one of us got kidnapped and impersonated by pod people or alien shapeshifters. Unfortunately, I never told you my passwords, so you're just going to have to take my word for it.'

Julie tucked her head into the crook of Aisling's neck, laughing, halfway between mirth and relief. 'You are *such* a nerd,' she gasped out.

'I also have a contingency plan in case zombies attack while I'm alone at home,' said Aisling. 'Can I have my phone back?'

'Yeah,' said Julie, pulling away a little but not letting go, even though it meant rooting around in her bag and giving back the phone one-handed.

The seagulls were clustered in a circle at one side of the room, whispering furiously amongst themselves. The Queen-that-is and the Queen-that-will-be were standing facing each other, such utter loathing on each of their faces that Julie could almost feel it radiating off them. Molly Red was staring at the two queens, for once looking alert and interested rather than nonchalant.

'What have you done?' said the Queen-that-will-be. 'What have you done to the City?'

'I have made it better,' said the Queen-that-is. 'I have made it safe!'

'You have twisted it beyond recognition and drained it of all its life!' said the Queen-that-will-be. 'I cannot let this stand. I challenge you!'

'Accepted! I will defeat you, as I defeated the third of us, and you will suffer as she suffered.'

Molly Red had somehow made her way over to Julie's side without making a noise. She tugged on Julie's elbow.

'They're distracted,' she said. 'We'd best leave them to it before they start throwing things and breaking glass. They're not interested in us now.'

She opened the door, and Julie and Aisling went through it, Julie glancing back to see the two queens circling each other, spitting words like venom, as the seagulls watched nervously.

'What's with the birds?' said Julie as they passed through the second set of doors and headed for the stairs. 'Why are they acting so shifty?'

'I think they don't know whose side to be on,' said Aisling. 'They're supposed to be loyal to the queen, but what does that mean when the queens are fighting amongst themselves?'

'If they side with one of them, will that mean she wins?' said Julie.

'If they side with the Queen-that-will-be, it'll even up the fight, so it's anyone's guess who'll come out on top,' said Molly Red. 'If they side with the Queen-that-is, she'll most likely win.'

Julie stopped dead. 'What? But then – we have to go back, we have to help her! We can't let the Queen-that-is win! We swore an oath!'

Molly Red shrugged. 'Your oath was to leave the City of the Three Castles with a better ruler than you found it with. That could still happen, even if the Queen-that-is wins this duel.'

Now it was Aisling's turn to stop dead. 'How do you know that?' she said quietly.

'How do you know it's not true?' said Molly Red. 'Anything's possible. No matter how strong she is, she's not invincible, and as the City weakens, she will weaken too.'

'No, I mean, how do you know what oath we took. I didn't tell you about it. Did you?' she said, turning to Julie.

Julie shook her head and looked at Molly Red, who was standing still on the stairs below them, facing forward. 'I suppose the – the Queen of Crows might have told you?'

Molly Red turned, just her head, and nodded sharply. 'That she might have.'

'But she didn't, did she?' said Aisling. 'You didn't need her to, because you already knew. Because you were the one who made us swear it in the first place.'

Molly Red grinned, and her body vanished, and her head transformed into the wrinkled floating head that had opened the door of the house to them. 'If you were any sharper, you'd cut yourself,' she said in the raspy voice of the head-of-the-house, then transformed back. 'I needed help, and there was nobody else in the City I could count on,' she said. 'Most of the City's own people had disappeared or were too afraid of the queen to make a noise. And you – you have your own selves well in hand, do you follow me? You know who you are, and you can't be swayed into being anyone else, oath or no oath.'

'You get around, don't you?' said Aisling. 'How many of the other people in the City were really you in disguise?'

Molly Red had opened her mouth to answer when a thought occurred to Julie. 'We could do what we liked, then, couldn't we?' she said, thinking aloud. 'Because … we're not from this place, and it – the rules don't have the same sway over us. Do they?'

'No,' said Molly Red, nodding in agreement, 'not the same sway at all.'

Aisling gave Julie a startled look. 'That … yes, that makes sense,' she said. To Molly Red, she said, 'So we could break the oath we made? I mean, it wouldn't … we wouldn't find ourselves forced into anything. We could just … not do it.'

'Yes,' said Molly Red. 'You could.'

There was a pause. Julie bit her lip, not sure whether to feel more cheated or guilty or relieved. She could have stopped herself from killing that seagull after all, if she had fought the urge. If she had known she *could* fight the urge. (But it must have come back by now. It was the way things worked in this place. So did it count as 'killing', really?)

'Are you going to?' said Molly Red, casually, as if it were an afterthought, not something that greatly concerned her.

Julie looked at Aisling, who was looking at her. Aisling nodded, and Julie thought she understood. They were on the same side. They were in this together. They wanted the same thing, in more ways than one.

Julie squeezed Aisling's hand and looked at Molly Red.

'No,' she said. 'We'll see this through.' From the corner of her eye she could see Aisling nodding, and it gave her a warm feeling.

'I thought you would,' said Molly Red. 'Now, we need to take care of our plan B, in case the wrong queen wins.'

'What's this "we" business, paleface?' Julie muttered.

'Wait,' said Aisling. 'Do you know about the dam on the River? The Ferryman wanted me to ask you.'

Molly Red frowned, then grinned and snapped her fingers. 'Brilliant! The River! That'll take care of it!'

'What river?' said Julie. 'There was a river in the City before, where the Liffey would have been, but it's gone now.'

'Because the Queen of Crows dammed up the

Ferryman's River,' said Molly Red, 'so that the Lord of Shadows couldn't use it to travel through the Realms Between.'

'Who *is* this Ferryman?'

'Think Charon,' said Aisling, grim-faced. 'And Styx. Not that that's the River's name, but it gets the idea across.'

'Oh,' said Julie. There were so many questions she wanted to ask, but Aisling didn't look like she wanted to talk about whatever had happened to her after she'd … died, or almost died. 'I suppose … she's the Queen of Death, so it stands to reason she'd have control over the River to the afterlife –'

'She doesn't,' said Molly Red, interrupting. 'The River is older and greater than she is. She was able to dam it up because it passed through her lands, but it's not bound to her any more than you are. And if we set it free, it's going to be really pissed off.'

'But it'll be pissed off at the Queen of Crows, right? We want to take care of herself upstairs, not the Queen of Crows. She's not even here in the City any more.'

'Oh, we don't need to worry about that,' said Molly Red, smiling.

Aisling rolled her eyes. 'Is this the part where you tell us to trust you?' she said.

'It's the part where you don't have a choice,' said Molly Red. 'Come on, follow me, and I'll take you to the place where the River was dammed.'

She leapt away down the stairs and, after a brief exchange of glances, Julie and Aisling followed her.

'Are you all right?' Julie murmured when she was sure Molly Red was out of earshot. 'You seemed like … You've been … You scared me.'

'I never knew you cared,' said Aisling.

'Neither did I,' said Julie. 'Turns out I do, which, you know, I'm as surprised as you are about.'

'You're still holding my hand.'

'Yes, I am. Is that a problem?'

'No! No, not at all. Just an observation.'

'But seriously,' Julie said, '*are* you all right?'

'I'm fine,' said Aisling. 'Or I will be. It's all a bit … Did you ever get the flu and have one of those really vivid dreams? This whole trip has been like that. What happened after I got hit on the head wasn't all that different from all the other things that have happened. Which maybe sounds improbable, but you've been here, you've seen what it's like. Well, the River, the Ferryman, all that – it's the same kind of thing.'

'I read a book once where Fairyland and the Land of the Dead were the same place.'

'So did I,' said Aisling. 'This isn't that, I think. But … it's like different levels on a video game? Even if there's a level that's a dream sequence, it's all part of the same game. The place I … went to, or whatever, was like … another one of the Realms Between.'

'Do you think … when people die in, in mortal

realms, that they – they go wherever you went?'

Aisling seemed to chew on that thought for a while. 'I don't know,' she said at last. 'I don't think so. Or if they do, they probably don't see it the way I saw that place.'

Julie let that thought sit for a while as they followed Molly Red down the corridors of the Tower and out through the courtyard and past the gates. The guards didn't try to stop them, seeming too dazed to move. Molly Red led them south, to the place where, in Dublin, O'Connell Street turned into O'Connell Bridge.

'This is where the River was,' said Julie. 'Before … well, before. It's where it ought to be.'

Molly Red nodded. 'What do you see, Aisling?' she said.

Aisling frowned. 'What are you – oh. Oh!'

'What?' said Julie. 'What is it? What can you see?'

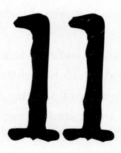

11

Aisling blinked rapidly and rubbed her eyes to make sure there was nothing caught in them, that she wasn't just seeing floaters or afterimages. She tried to say, 'What on earth is going on?' but only the first word came out, and it was an incomprehensible croak. She cleared her throat and tried again.

'You tell me,' she said, staring. 'What *am* I seeing?'

There were hundreds of little black filaments floating in the air, light as spiderwebs and twice as delicate.

'Only those who have crossed the River can see them,' said Molly Red. 'I don't know if they have a name. I've seen them a few times, though not as often as those who are born in the Fae Kingdoms and treat crossing the River like crossing their own front doorstep. You may be the first mortal ever to see them, for all I know.'

'But what *are* they?' said Aisling, her eyes still caught by the threads, which seemed to wink in and out of existence as she watched them, in a pattern she thought she would recognise if she had more time to watch.

'They are little threads in the tapestry of fate,' said Molly Red. 'If you can see them, you can catch hold of them, and they'll take you to the Ferryman's domain. But whatever you do when you're there, you'll have to be quick. You won't be able to see them for long, and I don't know how many times a mortal can cross the River before she stops being mortal.'

'What about you and Julie?' said Aisling. 'Will you be left behind?'

'Not bloody likely,' said Julie, slipping her hand from Aisling's and sliding it up to grab her elbow instead. 'If you're going, I'm going. I'm not letting you out of my sight until we're back home!'

Aisling gave Julie a small grateful smile and squeezed her hand where it was resting in the crook of her elbow. 'If you hold on to me, maybe – maybe you'll come along?'

Molly Red shrugged. 'Maybe. Why not? It's worth a try. But whatever you do, do it quickly.'

'OK,' said Aisling. She looked around her at the black filaments, dancing in the air. There were so many of them, it was almost as if a dark rain were falling from the sky or a dark mist rising up from the ground.

'On three,' she said, spotting one that seemed to be hanging around for longer than the others. 'One. Two.' She felt Molly Red touching her shoulder. 'Three!'

Aisling closed her hand around the thread, and as she did she felt a sort of jolt – like when a rollercoaster car drops down from its highest point – and everything went white, just as it had when she'd passed through the mist with the Queen-that-will-be. When her vision cleared, she was standing with Julie and Molly Red on the same hillside she had found herself on before, in the valley where the River flowed, except that the River had dried down to a trickle, barely even a stream.

There was a man sitting despondently on the hillside, staring at what had once been a river with an expression of utter and complete melancholy. As they came closer, Aisling recognised him.

'Well, hello there,' she said. 'I wondered what would happen to you.'

Morgan de Meath looked up, and his expression lightened a little.

'Greetings,' he said, rising to his feet. 'I hope your presence here does not mean your mission failed?'

'We're not done with it yet,' said Julie.

Morgan looked at Molly Red, and Molly Red looked back at him.

'Did you know,' he said, 'that the River would not lend the Ferryman's fee to me, as a servant of the Queen of Crows?'

'I had an inkling,' said Molly Red. 'I thought I might need you. And I do. Have you had time to think about what I told you?'

'I am still sworn to the Queen of Crows,' said Morgan. 'I cannot disobey her.'

'Yes, you can,' said Aisling. 'If it's true that you're a mortal, you're not really bound by those oaths. You can fight them.'

Morgan looked alarmed, as if the foundations of his world were shaking. 'Fight them? Can such a thing be?'

'How do you think I became known as the Oathbreaker?' said Molly Red.

He looked away, at the dwindling river and the hills and the valley. 'Is it true, then, what you said? That I had mortal parents?'

'Yes,' said Molly Red. She stepped closer, touching his arm, a gentle expression on her face. 'You were born in a mortal realm, and your parents are still alive. You have sisters who have never known you. You can find them again, but only if you break with the Queen of Crows. She means you no good. She means no good to the Realms Between. You must see that by now.'

Morgan blinked and breathed heavily, as if he were fighting tears, and nodded.

'I have served her faithfully, not because I chose it,

but because I thought there was no choice. Now, you offer me a choice, and I choose to rebel. The Queen of Crows has no more hold on me.'

At those words, he shivered all over, as if he had been doused with cold water. He faced the three of them with a new light in his eyes.

'Now,' he said, 'how may I help you in thwarting her plans?'

'There's a dam on the River,' said Aisling. 'What do you know about that?'

'I was the one to build it,' said Morgan. 'At the queen's command, of course.'

'Of course,' said Aisling. 'Well, take us to it and help us to destroy it. Then I reckon the Ferryman'll be so grateful he'll let you across the River without a fare. Or the River will be so grateful it'll let you cross without using the ferry. Either way, you'll be back in the lands of the living, and the Queen of Crows will have had one of her plans foiled.'

'But hurry,' added Julie. 'We don't have much time. We have to get back while Aisling can still see the threads of fate.'

Morgan gave Aisling a sharp look and nodded, as if he knew exactly what Julie was talking about from first-hand experience.

'Follow me,' he said and started to sprint upriver along the hillside.

They followed him, keeping pace easily – more easily than Aisling expected; every few strides, it seemed she bumped into a sort of warp in the air, like a heat-haze, which propelled her forward faster than she'd ever be able to move normally. The River was a blur to her left, and all she was aware of as she ran was the ground beneath her feet and the shapes of Julie and Molly Red at either side and Morgan de Meath ahead of her.

A long way and a short time later, Morgan slowed and came to a stop, and Aisling skidded to a halt beside him.

'There,' he said, pointing up. The valley sloped upwards from where they stood, and at its highest point there was a ramshackle wooden structure bridging the River and blocking it, letting only a thin trickle of water come through.

'It's big,' said Julie.

'The River's bigger,' said Aisling. 'If you want to destroy a dam, you don't need to *destroy* it. Weaken it a little, leave a crack or two, and the River will destroy it for you, and not slowly, either.'

She strode forward, scanning the dam for any weak points. It looked very shaky indeed from a distance, but the closer she got, the more she could see how carefully it had been constructed, every block and plank of wood fitting neatly in with all the others. 'This might be tricky,' she said when Julie came up by her side. 'It's not a bad bit of construction. Better than I was expecting.'

Julie tilted her head to one side. 'Don't you think it looks like a Jenga set?'

Aisling looked again. 'Huh,' she said, 'now that you mention it, yeah, it does.'

Julie made a smug face and cracked her knuckles. 'Step aside and watch the master at work,' she said.

Aisling watched as Julie clambered on top of the dam, hanging down from one of the higher protrusions at an alarming angle.

'Is that safe?' Aisling cried out.

'It's really solid!' Julie called back as she grabbed on to a lower-down block of wood and started easing it out of position. 'But it's not held together by anything. No nails or glue or anything, just the bits of wood and gravity.' The block eased all the way free and she pushed it down to float on the trickle that was all that remained of the River. A gush of water came through the hole that the block left in the dam, and she climbed backwards and down to a lower level.

'Come over here and give me a hand,' she said, and Aisling rushed over to help.

Together, they eased out three more blocks of wood, letting more and more water come through, until the trickle was a genuine stream once more. 'I think that's enough,' said Aisling. 'We should get to the bank before –'

There was a cracking, roaring sound, and Aisling reached for Julie's hand instinctively. The River swelled up and rushed towards them, knocking them off the dam and washing them down, down, down, and away, away from where the dam had been, away from the valley, away from Morgan de Meath and Molly Red.

Aisling kept a firm grip on Julie's hand and tried not to panic. *I already died once*, she thought, *and it wasn't so bad.* The water was rushing all around her, those screaming faces everywhere she looked, but she was just about able to keep her head above it, and through the choppy waves she caught glimpses of Julie, still with her head above water, though her face was pale and shocked.

Just as the water seemed to be calming down, there was a strange, sickening lurch, and the water lifted them impossibly high. There was a wave even higher in front of them, and the wave was not wave-shaped but took the form of a woman with flowing hair, a blankly peaceful face, and legs so long and curvy that they looked faintly freakish. She looked familiar, though Aisling couldn't put words on why.

'Anna Livia,' Julie whispered, her hand gripping Aisling's like a vice.

The river-woman did not open her mouth, and her expression did not change, but a sound came from her like the rushing of water, and in that sound were words:

YOU HAVE FREED ME. WHAT IS YOUR WISH?

'Um,' said Aisling, her mind blank.

Julie looked at her and then looked at the river-woman. 'We don't really have a wish, I suppose. Oh! Could you bring us back to the City of the Three Castles? Is that –'

I WILL, said the river-woman. Her body dissolved back into a river, and the high wave that had lifted the two of them subsided slowly, though not so slowly that it was comfortable. They were being pulled along, now, by a current too strong to fight.

Aisling closed her eyes and held tight to Julie's hand.

There was a great swell in the River, and the two of them were deposited on land that, if not exactly dry, was at least solid. Aisling took a deep breath, and another, and another, and opened her eyes.

They were back in the City of the Three Castles, on a stretch of street that would have been O'Connell Bridge in Dublin, and though it had let them fetch up on the bank, the River had not stopped its flow but was surging northwards up the street that was not quite O'Connell Street, once more taking the form of a giant woman.

Julie pushed her soaking wet hair out of her eyes with the hand that wasn't holding Aisling's hand. 'Should we ...' She trailed off, staring at the River.

'Let's see what happens, at least,' said Aisling. 'Even

if we can't do anything about it. Let's see how the story ends.'

Julie nodded, and in perfect step they walked in the River's wake towards the Tower.

'What do you think will happen to Molly Red and that guy?' said Julie as they passed the O'Connell Monument.

'I don't know,' said Aisling, 'but I'm not worried. Molly Red knows her way around these parts. In fact, I wouldn't be surprised if this was all part of her plan.'

The River was making a roaring, rushing noise as it surged up the street, and it seemed to change the very bricks and tarmac and concrete it passed over, wiping them away and transforming them to cobblestones that flickered in and out of existence, before settling back into bricks and tarmac and concrete, as if different eras of the street's history were battling for supremacy. The railings around the Tower dissolved into nothing as the River approached it, and the horse-headed guards threw their heads back and neighed, high pitched and frightened sounding, before changing into horses with rope bridles on their heads and galloping away as fast as their legs could carry them.

WHERE IS THE QUEEN? said the River.

Its head was level with the top floor of the Tower. From the ground, Aisling could see flashes of light that looked like bolts of electricity, but no detail. The flashes slowed down and stopped, and the Tower

271

seemed to shrink a little, and a balcony grew out of its side for the two queens to walk out on.

'What is your wish?' said one of them – Aisling couldn't tell which.

I AM OWED A BOON.

'Ask, then.'

TWO COINS BOUGHT YOUR LIFE, QUEEN-THAT-WILL-BE. I HAVE COME TO COLLECT THAT DEBT.

Aisling thought of the horse that had knocked her and Julie over, the horse that had had the Queen-that-will-be on its back; that horse had been Molly Red, and she had delivered the queen to the Ferryman's land without the fare to pay him. Was this what she had wanted all along? Had they been dancing to Molly Red's tune since the moment they caught that scent of wormwood?

'Yes!' cried a triumphant voice from the Tower's balcony. 'Yes, take her life! She is the one who owes you a boon – take her life from her now and leave the City to me!'

No, said the River. CENTURIES AGO, YOU SPLIT YOUR LIFE IN THREE TO FOOL ME, SO THAT YOUR RULE MIGHT LAST FOREVER. THERE IS NO IS, NO WAS, NO WILL-BE. YOU THREE ARE ONE LIFE AND I WILL HAVE THAT ONE LIFE FOR MY OWN.

'You cannot mean that, River!' said another voice, and this time Aisling was pretty sure it was the Queen-that-will-be speaking. 'I owe you a boon, I do not deny that, but do not ask for this! My sister does not owe you her life. I do not owe you my life!'

The Queen-that-was knows that for a lie, said the River. I have claimed her life already.

The body of the river-woman rippled and the faces blurred, and the River's hand changed shape so that a woman's form was standing on it – the form of the Queen-that-was, shaped out of the same rippling dark water as the River.

'The River speaks the truth,' said the Queen-that-was. 'Our time is done, my sisters, my selves. This trick we played on Death will last no longer. It is time.'

She dissolved back into the River, and the River moved closer to the Tower.

I have no power to compel you, it said. You are queen of your own domain, and in your domain only your own honour binds you. What does your honour say?

'We are three,' said the Queen-that-is. 'We are … we are …'

'We are one,' said the Queen-that-will-be. 'It is only your madness, sister, that has divided us. Until this late battle, we have always been one. That which binds one of us, binds all of us.'

Then your life is forfeit, said the River. Your life is mine.

'Our … our life is yours,' said the Queen-that-will-be.

The River surged forward, and it seemed that at the same time the two queens leapt from the balcony, hand in hand, and were swallowed by the writhing water, which surged back southwards in the form of a great wave and flowed back to the place where the Liffey should have been. Even the water soaking their clothes and hair leapt away from them to rejoin the wave, leaving them completely dry.

The Tower seemed to change again, shrinking inwards and growing metallic and shiny, until it was no longer a tower at all but had settled on a shape that was almost, but not quite, exactly the same as the Spire of Dublin.

The street was changing before their eyes, old buildings fading to be replaced by newer ones, which faded in their turn. It was still not quite O'Connell Street, and there were still very few smells and almost no people, but every so often there would be a flash of someone walking across the street or visible through a shop's front window, over in a matter of seconds, and none too solid while it happened, as if the city were populated by impatient ghosts.

'The gates must have opened,' said Julie, and Aisling nodded.

They started walking, away from what had been the Tower and was now the Spire. When they reached the southern end of the street, there was a bridge there that was very like O'Connell Bridge, though there was no boardwalk leading down the quays to either side, and the lampposts on the pavements didn't have any band stickers or political posters on them. Without saying a word, the two of them walked together to the east side of the bridge and leaned over. There were seagulls floating on the River, flying low over the surface, swooping into the water to catch fish.

A flock of pigeons descended on the parapet and started shuffling over towards them. The parapet was too narrow to accommodate more than one of them, so they had to walk in single file, which made them look like a troop of feathered schoolchildren following a lollipop lady across the road.

'Do you feel like we've left something undone?' said Aisling as she glanced between the pigeons and the seagulls.

Julie let go of Aisling's hand and slid her arm around Aisling's waist.

'Yeah, it feels unfinished,' she said. 'Like we made a shopping list and then left it at home. Milk, eggs, bread?'

Aisling put her arm around Julie's shoulders. It felt right, to stand like that. Julie fitted snugly under her arm, and if she tilted her head slightly she could bury her nose in Julie's hair; it smelled of something sweetish, probably hairspray. 'Whatever it is, I don't feel like going just yet,' she said. 'Though, now that I think of it, I'm not sure we can. We'd have to find the Wormwood Gate, wouldn't we?'

'I don't think so,' said Julie, gesturing at the ghostly figures dipping in and out of existence. 'Look at all the people coming and going. I'm guessing once the queens were gone, the gates all opened again, all at once. We can probably get back to Dublin just by following one of those people.'

'Good thinking,' said Aisling.

'I'm not just a pretty face,' said Julie.

'Though you *are* a pretty face,' said Aisling. 'I – I mean, you have a pretty face. I don't mean you literally are a face, I mean, that would be ridiculous, like, just imagine a face on legs, how weird would that be?'

'You are the most rubbish compliment-giver in the history of time,' said Julie. 'But you're not bad-looking yourself, you know.'

'Oh, really?'

'Yeah, you know, in a certain light.'

Kiss her, said a voice in Aisling's head. *Kiss her now, before you lose your nerve. Go on! She wants you to!*

She put her other hand on Julie's shoulder and turned her slightly. Julie was blushing a little; she tilted her head and gave Aisling a look that was equal parts expectant and challenging. Aisling leaned in.

'Oi! Yous two! We've got a bone to pick with yous!'

'Oh, bollocks,' Aisling muttered. Julie giggled, and they pulled apart from each other.

The pigeons were gathered in a row on the parapet in front of them, their chests all puffed up and their beady little eyes fixed on Julie.

'What is it?' said Aisling.

'I,' said one of the pigeons, the one closest to the two of them, 'am a seagull!'

Aisling and Julie exchanged baffled glances.

'No, you're not,' said Julie. 'you're a pigeon. Or, well, you certainly look like a pigeon. Are you under a spell or something? Disguised? And what does it have to do with us, anyway?'

'I've been a seagull through five hundred years and two hundred bleeding incarnations, and now look at me!' said the pigeon. 'It's all your fault!'

'Oh,' said Julie. 'You're the one I threw that stone at. I killed you, didn't I? When you were flying over the Viking quarter with your flock, looking for pigeons.'

'That you did,' said the seagull-turned-pigeon. 'And for all's I'd like to, I don't blame you for that. No, I blame you for when you did it! You caught me when the way through the labyrinth was dark as the inside of a dragon's arse, and the Ferryman wouldn't let me fly across the River. I had to take his ferry, and the only way he'd let me was if I gave him two feathers for a fare and let him choose what I'd be when I got back to the City. And now look at me! Is this his idea of a joke? Fine feckin' sense of humour he's got!'

'Is it really that bad?' said Aisling. 'At least you're

still a bird. You could have been reincarnated as a worm, or an ant, or a cockroach.'

'I'd rather be a cockroach than a feckin' pigeon!' said the former seagull. 'Grubby little dirt-eaters, the flock of them!'

'I can see how this must be distressing for you,' said Aisling, 'but I'm not sure I understand what you think we can do about it.'

'Take him away!' said another pigeon, and the rest cooed in agreement, rustling their wings. 'He's been bellyaching since he came back from the River's banks about how he's not meant to be a pigeon, and we're feckin' sick of it. Take him with yous when you go, and let him complain as much as he likes to the pigeons over there!'

'I don't think that's a good solution,' said Julie. 'You'll still be miserable. You need to either find a way to change back into a seagull or get so you're not bothered about being a pigeon. I'm sure, with time, you can get used to it. And then, the next time you die, I'm sure you'll be able to come back as a seagull.'

'I don't want to wait that long!' said the former seagull. "N' anyway, these flocking dirt-eaters don't like me any more than I like them. But me own kind won't let me join them. "Can you swim?" they say. Can I swim! Do I look like I can feckin' swim?'

'You know,' said Aisling, 'all this hostility is bad for you. Bad for the pigeons, and bad for the seagulls too. I realise you guys have short lives and it probably seems like you've been at war forever, but you haven't, not really. And now that the queens have left the City, there's no reason for you to be at odds with each other.'

'Exactly!' said Julie. 'And someone like yourself, who's seen both sides of the issue – you could be a go-between. An ambassador between the two great bird tribes.'

The seagull-turned-pigeon shuffled from side to side, its chest puffing up a little.

'Ambassador? Ambassador. I like that. Like the sound of it. 'S got a ring to it.'

'Yes, and then, if you join together, you birds could rule the City. There's no one to stand in your way,' said Aisling.

Julie grinned at her. 'Good thinking,' she said quietly, and Aisling grinned back.

The pigeons started cooing and shuffling, as if they were giving the matter some thought.

'A parliament!' one of them called out. 'At the base of the Tower. As soon as you can. Summon all the pigeons of the City. And you, fishbreath, tell the seagulls they're invited too. We'll see if we can't rule the City better than the one-eyed triplets.'

'You could hardly do worse,' said Aisling, and as the pigeons rose from the parapet in unison, she felt a sudden lightness and ease descend on her.

'That was it,' said Julie. 'That was the thing we were supposed to do.'

'Well, we swore to leave the City with a better ruler,' said Aisling. 'I guess politics really is for the birds.' Julie slapped her hard on the arm. 'Ow! What was that for?'

'Conditioning,' said Julie. 'I'm not going out with you if you make bad puns.'

'Oh,' said Aisling. 'So … we're going out, are we?'

'No,' said Julie, looking around. 'I mean –'

She grabbed Aisling's hand and darted away, following a woman who had appeared out of nowhere, and dragging Aisling after her. There was a shift in air pressure and a sudden increase of noise, and then they had slipped out of the City of the Three Castles and back into Dublin – the real O'Connell Bridge, in the real Dublin – as easily as taking a step over the threshold of a house.

Aisling stood very still and stared and let the sounds and smells of the city assault her. She could hear the roaring of cars and fragments of a dozen conversations and the beeping of the pedestrian-crossing signals; she could smell exhaust fumes and dried urine and hops wafting over from James's Gate. It was like being yanked out of a sensory deprivation tank in the middle of an air raid, or like stepping out of a line drawing into reality. She felt a little dizzy, and though she'd been on the verge of saying or doing something before they'd moved, she couldn't remember what it was.

She checked her phone. It was 9.27 pm, on the same night it had been when they fell through the Wormwood Gate.

'Hey,' said Julie, letting go of her hand and stepping in close.

Aisling dropped her phone into her pocket and looked down at her. Julie's face was upturned, a little anxious, a little excited.

Oh, I remember now, she thought and leaned down and kissed her.

Julie slid her hands around Aisling's waist, inside her coat. Aisling shivered, though she felt warm all over, from the inside out. She rested her hands on the back of Julie's neck and pulled away, reluctantly.

'So,' she said, 'you were saying?'

'I don't think it was important,' said Julie.

They stared at each other, grinning like idiots. Aisling wanted to come up with some clever line, something funny and sweet that they'd always remember, that would be their own personal in-joke for months and years to come, but the soundtrack of her mind was nothing but trumpets and a chorus of *yesyesyesyesyesyesyesYES!* and, under those conditions, it was impossible to be witty.

'So,' she said eventually, 'do you want to rejoin the party?'

Julie gave her a funny look. 'No,' she said. 'I think we've done enough for one night, don't you?'

'Oh, yeah,' said Aisling. 'Nightclubs are going to seem a bit dull in comparison to overthrowing an ancient monarchy and surfing on a river of drowned souls.'

Julie sighed heavily and hugged her. 'Thank God,' she said, 'I was beginning to think you'd forgotten. That we'd both forget, as if it never happened.'

Aisling hugged her back. 'That's impossible,' she said. 'I am never, ever going to forget tonight.'

Julie pulled back and kissed her lightly on the mouth. 'Me neither,' she said. 'For more than one reason.'

She grabbed Aisling's hand and ran away, and Aisling ran with her, laughing, dodging and weaving past the people, her feet lighter than air and her heart lighter still.

ACKNOWLEDGEMENTS

Big thanks to Siobhán Parkinson and Elaina O'Neill of Little Island for their editorial advice and unflagging enthusiasm. Thanks also to Little Island's anonymous manuscript-reviewers, who made an invaluable contribution.